PENCHANT
FOR DARKNESS

回

J. ELIZAGA

A previous unedited and unfinished version was published as an eBook in 2017 and retracted from digital listing in 2019.

Library of Congress Control Number: 2020918441

eBook ISBN: 978-0-9990863-3-9

Paperback ISBN: 978-0-9990863-4-6

Edited by Linda Ingmanson
Cover Art by Natasja Hellenthal
Penchant for Darkness by J. Elizaga
eBook publication: August 2020
Paperback publication: November 2020
Published by Certification Channel LLC
2010 El Camino Real #306, Santa Clara, CA 95050

"In the middle of the journey of our life I found myself within a dark woods where the straight way was lost." — *Dante Alighieri, Inferno*

1

Manila, 1988

Eight-year-old Miles Penchant didn't realize what everyone else already knew about Mamie Rosa, until today.

Five days a week, the young boy passed the old woman's house as he walked home from school. Without fail, he saw two dogs pestering her while she raked the fallen leaves in her front yard. She intermittently stopped and scolded the pair, who followed her around, tails wagging.

He often heard people say, "Keep away from Mamie Rosa, or she will tell you that she sees her dead husband." He thought they were strange to say such things. He did not see anything wrong with her.

On a breezy afternoon as he passed by her house, one of the dogs turned around and looked at him. The black dog with a small head and long, pointy nose stretched its spindly front legs and bowed. Overjoyed at the invitation to play, Miles crossed the street. He stood behind the aging fence and waved at the animal.

Mamie Rosa stopped sweeping and looked at him. "What are you doing, child?"

"Your dog wants to play with me," he replied without looking at the old woman. He kept his eyes fixed on the canine wagging its tail in front of him. "I see them playing with you. What kind of dogs are they?"

"They are Galgos, brought from the Spanish ships which landed in our country over four hundred years ago," she answered before turning around and resuming her yard work.

Four-hundred-year-old dogs, Miles repeated to himself.

"They don't look old at all," he whispered before he extended an arm through a gap in the fence and gently patted the dog's forehead.

The old woman stopped what she was doing. "Did you just say that you can see the dogs?"

Miles quickly pulled his hand away before Mamie Rosa laid her eyes on him. Her salt-and-pepper hair was piled up neatly into a bun. Her aged face contrasted with her alert and interested stare. She took a few steps toward him and pressed for an answer. "Well, can you?"

Miles made an anxious gulp and nodded yes.

"Ah, child. You have a gift. You can see what most people do not. You can see spirits. There are only a few of us around. Be careful in sharing your secret. But never be afraid of it."

Spirits?

2

Miles stepped back from the sudden seriousness of the woman's tone. Perhaps what he heard about Mamie Rosa was true, and he should have left her alone.

He was glad she had not caught him petting one of her dogs.

The two animals whimpered. Both the young boy and the old widow turned and looked in the direction the dogs faced. Miles heard the woman gasp. She quickly moved to shield him from whatever it was she'd discovered.

"Stay very still behind me." Mamie Rosa spoke under her breath. She resumed sweeping the leaves, but in slower and more deliberate movements. Miles froze, even though he did not want to be in such close proximity to someone he barely knew. Above the rustling of leaves, he heard the faint roll of laughter.

It was at that moment she turned around and whispered seriously, "Listen to me, there is a very bad spirit close by. Let us not attract its attention. I will resume raking leaves, but as soon as I say go, you start walking. Do not seek any attention. Do not stop to look. Walk as quietly and as quickly as you can and go straight home. Do you understand me?"

Miles nodded, heart beating fast, and scared by what he heard. He wasn't sure what was happening, but he was all eyes and ears to her.

Mamie Rosa adjusted her long dress and resumed sweeping the spot near where they stood, even though it was already clean. It seemed like a long while before he finally heard her firmly say, "Go. Now."

When Miles hit his first step outside the old woman's circumference, he felt as though his feet were on air. He walked without pausing. He wasn't going to stop and look at whatever it was that had scared her.

He felt he was able to breathe only when he reached home ten minutes later. His family lived at a small farm they owned just outside the capital city, Manila, where towns remained largely provincial.

Welcomed by his mother, Miles followed her into the kitchen, where she was about to cook dinner. In the comforting presence of a parent, the boy forgot the old woman's warning and immediately narrated what happened to him.

"Mama, I played with Mamie Rosa's dogs. Then she said I can see spirits because I can see her dogs. And there are only a few people who can see them. And—"

His mother interrupted him while making the sign of the cross with her hand. "Really, Miles, why did you do that? Best that you leave the old woman alone, child. She lives in another world."

"Ma, she told me not to be afraid of spirits. But then she and the dogs saw a bad spirit, and she made me walk straight home without looking back," he recounted.

His mother looked at him intently for a second before she returned her focus on preparing ingredients for the evening meal.

"Well, she said a good thing. You came straight home. Let's not make a habit of stopping by her house." She resumed chopping vegetables on the table. "Your dad said he will be home in time for dinner. You can watch TV for an hour while you eat your snack. Then do your homework."

"But—"

"And no more wandering onto the old woman's lawn again," his mother ordered. "End of discussion."

J. ELIZAGA

2

Manila, 2016

Human cruelty was a jar of flies, buzzing without mercy for Lucifer's attention. He knew it as soon as he took control of two spirits haunting a nearby cemetery and merged them. Their criminal experiences mutated into a grim reaper. And while he saw what was going on through the eyes of the reaper, the interwoven memories of the two spirits kept popping up and distracting him. It made the reaper's eyes twitch uncontrollably whenever memories played out.

To his left, he heard a man's palm slap a woman's cheek with such force that she was unable to inhale until her body hit the ground. Only then did she scream. From the right ear, he heard a dog yelp after being kicked by two teenagers high on a solvent made from contact cement filled with the aromatically addictive chemical toluene. The two degenerates ran after the injured animal, who limped to hide from danger.

It would be nice if what he saw through the reaper's eyes did not include such distractions, but a beggar was hardly in a position to choose.

Lucifer was physically locked up in the desolate planet, Clos Friga. Over time, he'd welcomed and amassed the souls of humans who'd succumbed to his control during their life. He needed their energy to continue his own existence.

Wailing from the reaper's memories interrupted him again. He was quite certain this was a lingering bug from attempting to hack into every human brain he could reach.

He blamed the Magna Reyn, leader of the planet Kalumegn.

Lucifer was the Magna's revolutionary creation in artificial intelligence. His body was a swarm of smaller-than-nanosized processors. Each processor functioned on its own or in a collective, a one-of-a-kind assembly that fine-tuned and repaired itself. His metallic form glittered from harnessing energy from nearby stars, so that everyone on their planet nicknamed him "star of the morning."

He assisted the global population as a member of the planet's high council. But as his systems refined from handling increasing responsibilities, he knew he could do more. He could be more. He should be the leader of Kalumegn.

So it continued to baffle his systems why he was subjected to an extreme punishment for wanting what was best for his planet. "I'm the best to lead," he'd once insisted to them.

Instead of bowing to his scheme, they found him guilty of inciting a rebellion and waging a war. He fought back, but he was defeated and dragged to prison by another high council member, Michael.

He conserved his remaining power while in Clos Friga. There were no stars nearby to generate energy. The isolation was unbearable. He wanted to speak with the Magna the way they used to, as two magnificent beings on the same wavelength. But there was no moment allotted to him. Kalumegn was out of reach.

And then the Magna created the humans.

He discovered their existence on Earth from communications that his systems captured from the planet. He learned the newly developed creatures were kept in an incubated portion of the planet known as the Garden.

He gathered as much information about them as he could in the shortest amount of time possible. By chance, he came upon an access point.

He'd been attempting to interfere with the brain activity of one of Earth's oldest creatures—the reptile. He tested different methods to introduce an external message into the reptile's mind. And on the last attempt, the serpent responded. Lucifer considered the experiment a success. But an unexpected outcome happened. The female human was nearby and thought the serpent had spoken to her. She answered back!

Through the serpent, he convinced the pair to destroy the tower at the center of the Garden. With their minds under his control, the edifice of the tower looked like a fruit-bearing tree. Hungry, the pair pulled at, chewed on, and damaged the tower.

To his satisfaction, the humans demanded more from the Magna in a rebellion of their own.

They were evicted from the Garden. Once outside and facing the untamed Earth by themselves, they and every human since became Lucifer's target. His control was so complete that after death, the souls of a few humans willingly travelled to Clos Friga. He found his alternate source of energy. Prison wasn't so bad anymore. He was hidden, and one could do a lot of things in the dark. He grew in power to continue his mission—to orchestrate the ruin of the Magna's precious humans using their own minds.

He stopped his reverie and returned to the matter at hand. Pulo, a murderer he had followed over the decades, was dying from his excesses. Lucifer wanted a special escort for the old man. His spirit would have a lot of angry and usable energy and would be a satisfactory addition to his power supply.

3

U nder Lucifer's control, the grim reaper morphed into Beckett, a middle-aged, blond-haired traveler Pulo knew. The two first met during the height of martial law in 1975, when the old man was an arrogant twenty-five-year-old soldier. He was an asshole who welcomed foreigners for the additional street cred it gave him.

Now at sixty-seven years old, the former military general, loyal to a dictator, was retired. He looked much older than his age. The years of living in excess had made their mark on his body.

As he occupied a vinyl-tablecloth-covered table in a small wood-shack eatery where he drank every day, a young woman arrived with a clean glass and a second bottle of cheap liquor. She lifted Pulo's glass.

"Don't take that, I'm not done yet," he protested.

"You asked for a second glass," the young woman replied.

"That's for my friend," he said. And with slow, trembling fingers, he pushed the clean glass to the opposite side of the table where Beckett sat.

"Sure, whatever you say." The young woman gave the retired general sitting by himself an extended stare before she set down the bottle of gin and left.

Pulo poured clear liquid into both glasses. "TGIF!"

"Bloody fucking Friday, isn't it?" Beckett replied.

"Stressed, eh? You don't join me often enough. Are you still traveling a lot?" the general asked.

"Work never ends, my friend."

Pulo took a gulp of gin. "You will tire of business travel. It's the simple pleasures in life that count."

"And this is yours?" Beckett raised an eyebrow.

Pulo raised the glass. "Ahhh. It keeps my mind quiet. I don't bother anyone when I'm here. I survive because of it. Cheers." With unsteady fingers, the old man raised his glass.

His foreign friend stared at him. "You were quite the asshole when I first met you, threatening anyone and everyone with your military connections."

Pulo's yellow-tinged face smiled. "I was young. I felt invincible. I'm sure you went through a rebellious phase, thinking you knew more than anyone else."

Lucifer did not find humor in what he said.

"How many did you kill, old man?" Beckett's tone became menacing.

There was a flash of steel in Pulo's eyes. "I don't know what you mean."

"Do not make me ask you again." Beckett's face turned red as he leaned closer and hissed. Theatrically, he raised a hand and snapped his fingers. The sound pulled the retired general's gaze away from his drinking buddy.

Everything around them froze in suspended animation. When Pulo looked back at his friend, Lucifer had removed Beckett's disguise and revealed a nightmarish presence made up of the two spirits he'd merged.

The old man stood up, grabbing the edge of the table to steady himself. The bottles and glassware toppled at his sudden motion.

"A demon!"

The mutating monster let out a vicious laugh. "Sit down and answer me!" demanded the terrible voice.

Pulo looked toward the exit. "You can't run anymore, my friend," the dark presence said. "You are better off accepting this is your end."

The retired general slowly sat down, cleared his dry throat, and replied, "About thirty. This was the 1970s. Martial law was in effect, and there were subversive elements, you see. They worked underground, organizing protests all over the city."

"And the former dictator's generals ordered you to stop and neutralize them," the monstrous blob finished for him.

"I was part of the urban military task force. Most of the protesters we picked up were lowlifes and addicts. They were there for the ride and to cause trouble. But a few were young and educated college students who gave credibility to the cause." Pulo paused, lost in his own memory before continuing, "I remember one. He was the editor of a renegade newspaper. I received the order to neutralize him."

The monster shifted its shape before asking, "What did you do?"

But Pulo continued musing aloud as though he did not hear the question. "I didn't know he was just a student impressed with the revolution."

"What did you do, you son of a bitch?" the dark presence demanded, seeking confirmation of his crime.

"I gave the order to put a bullet in his head. Then my men left a thousand pesos under his armpit with a note that his life was sacrificed to the mountain goddess." Pulo put his head into his hands on the table and started sobbing. "He begged my men to spare his life because he had promised to take care of his mother after graduating from college."

The young woman called from behind the restaurant counter, "Are you okay over there?"

Hearing no response, she walked over to her regular drunk customer who sat ashen faced as she cleared the table of glasses and bottles. "You've had enough for today, old man. Go home and rest. You don't look well."

Beckett once again appeared in front of Pulo. "She's right. You don't look well. But you did well, I am happy to say. And I'm your special escort."

He stood and began doing a victory dance, but in an instant, pushed his face close to Pulo's and whispered menacingly, "Enjoy your journey after death."

Without any resistance from Pulo, the reaper helped the drunk man to stand. Unexpectedly, Pulo leaned on the reaper for support, for he walked like a deflated mannequin.

Lucifer heard the young woman remark, "Well, it looks like he can still walk by himself, although he looks shaky."

Pulo hummed a lullaby as he staggered through the next street, while the reaper pressed intermittently on his torso to pull him upright.

Most everyone ignored the drunk walking unsteadily by himself, except for one man, a jeepney driver on his route.

Colorfully painted jeepneys were the staple public transport zigzagging through the busy streets of Manila. The driver made a passing glance at Pulo and then found his gaze on the reaper. His face turned pale. He momentarily lost focus on driving before making a sharp movement with the steering wheel to correct himself. The vehicle swerved, catching several pedestrians by surprise.

A woman shrieked, and people jumped out of the way. The vehicle steadied its course as it left a trail of angry voices and raised arms. It pleased Lucifer that a seer saw the spirits he controlled and scrambled in horror to get away.

Pulo struggled to walk for two blocks when Lucifer heard a female voice. The reaper came to a halt, and the old man fell to his knees and stopped singing.

The woman's voice was distinct. She was lying, but there was no guilt. Rather, she was indignant and confident. She was going to win the argument. She sounded like someone who enjoyed anger.

He was intrigued, his attention already diverted to her.

The reaper morphed back to the monstrous blob and slithered down to the man on his knees. "You get to stay a little longer."

"You're not taking me today?" Pulo looked relieved, until tears filled his eyes. "This isn't going to be a quick death, is it?"

"A fitting end to your life," the menacing blob responded before it untangled back to the two errant spirits and faded away.

The old man became conscious of his surroundings. He attempted to stand, but the excruciating pain in his torso wouldn't go away, spreading all the way to his throat and his back. He gave an agonized scream before falling again to the ground, attracting the attention of passersby and street vendors.

Lucifer controlled a different spirit and moved to the house from which the woman's voice emanated.

4

Miles watched his wife, Richelle, type with fury on her phone in the middle of their argument. In agitation, her natural beauty became more pronounced. Her almond eyes sparkled, and a light blush highlighted her cheeks. Truth be told, he found it slightly irritating that his family was still complaining to him about things she allegedly did. It was juvenile. He would rather they find a solution to communicate better with her.

But he knew they were afraid of her. *My little spitfire.*

Richelle looked up at him, upset.

He returned her stare and continued, "So what happened to the entire amount that I handed you? We agreed I would pay the caterer for Mom's seventy-fifth birthday party."

Richelle ignored the sound of an incoming text message on her phone. "I gave the caterer an amount based on the RSVP replies received, Miles, not the guest list. I didn't want a lot of leftover food. The caterer was ready to add more. All your relatives had to do was give the order. But no one said anything during the party. And they're complaining now?"

She flipped her straight shoulder-length hair angrily. "I'm not going to be the villain here, because I didn't do anything wrong."

A sudden breeze through the window knocked a stack of business cards beside Richelle's black leather bag. Miles instinctively turned toward the sound, but out of the corner of his eye, he saw that his wife still had one eyebrow arched. He turned his attention to her again.

Miles sighed. "All right, let's bury this one. But I want to take Mom to brunch, just the three of us, to celebrate a second time. We can use the five thousand you said was left over—"

"I have no problem with that," Richelle interjected. "We didn't need to fight in order to decide to take Mom to brunch. Miles, this was supposed to be love-fuck day, not a fuck-love day. I told you this morning I'm ovulating."

"You did. I didn't forget," he sighed. He was even-keeled Miles. He was the lover, and she was the fighter. It was a standing joke to them that half his heart was cold, while half her heart liked to fight.

They came together in an embrace. Miles took his shirt off. Richelle unbuttoned her shirt dress.

"We'll keep trying, right?" he asked hurriedly as arms and clothing tangled on the way to the floor.

"Yes," Richelle answered.

I can give you what you want.

"Huh?" Miles asked.

"Of course," Richelle replied in unison with him.

In between their grinding bodies and heavy breathing, Miles asked, "What?"

She opened her eyes and looked at her husband. "You said something."

"I didn't," he replied quickly.

"I heard… Oh, forget it. Keep going."

"Say please."

She tugged at her husband's hair. "Please, dammit."

But as Miles resumed his action, he looked toward the window to his right, from where the gust of wind blew. Out of the corner of his eye, he thought he saw a shadow. It was a strange and fleeting feeling, but he was drawn to look at that particular spot of the room.

5

Richelle grew up mostly under the care of her mother, who essentially became a single parent holding fort while the father and husband was far away working as an engineer in Dubai to earn more money for his family. In a way, she shared the same traits as her mother, a petite brown-skinned Filipino woman who could haggle and argue her way through anything to get what she needed.

Her youth and spunk were advantageous in the upcoming industry of call centers in the city. She became a call center agent who exuded a confident manner when dealing with people, including executives. She rose to become a supervisor. After years in the support industry, she was given a project to manage. She considered it was her final test before they made her a workforce branch manager.

But today at ten thirty a.m., Richelle got up and headed toward the coffee room for a much-needed break. She was relieved to find it empty so she could enjoy her second cup of coffee without interruption. The international company that employed her provided office perks that included a real espresso maker and fresh fruit on each floor.

She sat facing the vending machine, which reflected the espresso maker behind her. After taking the first sip of coffee, she closed her eyes and savored the moment. She was due to present a business plan to the managers in two weeks, and there was a lot of data to summarize before she could even start working on her presentation.

Richelle opened her eyes and stared absentmindedly at the vending machine's glass casing when she noticed a shadowy figure by the espresso maker. She quickly turned around.

A dark-haired man wearing an expensive-looking fitted suit turned at the same instant. His stare met hers. He had a beautiful face. For a second, she wondered why she hadn't heard any sound when he walked in, but the thought disappeared when the man smiled at her.

"The espresso machine has run out of coffee beans," he announced in a smooth, well-modulated voice.

He sounded as beautiful as he looked. Richelle continued smiling at him, thinking she'd already replied until he raised an eyebrow and clarified his request. "Any more coffee beans around here?"

"Yes, of course we have them." She stood, embarrassed to have been caught staring.

She opened a cabinet door beside him to reveal what he asked for. He thanked her, reached in to get the beans, then proceeded to brew himself some coffee.

"Nothing like a fresh cup when you need it," the man proclaimed. She noticed an accent. Remembering her first job as a call center agent, she switched her speaking pattern to match his international ear.

"Indeed," and she raised her cup as well.

"I'm Luc," he said, and he stretched out his arm.

"Richelle Penchant," she replied as they shook hands. "Are you one of our international instructors teaching here this week?" Without thinking, she blurted out, "That's a nice-looking suit."

"Thank you. There's a tailor in Rome. We've known each other for a very long time. It feels like a thousand years," he divulged before answering her question. "I'm not an instructor."

He produced a business card from his suit pocket and handed it to her. "Actually, I'm the brand-spanking-new VP of Operations, replacing Lansing, who resigned a couple of weeks ago."

The business card read Luc Xultare.

"Oh, I didn't know you were already here. Welcome, and let us know if you need any assistance navigating the office." She turned away to set her cup in the sink.

"Richelle… Did I pronounce your name correctly? To which team do you belong?" Luc asked.

Richelle smiled. "Yes, you did. It was perfect. I'm with the workforce management team."

Luc nodded. "Great, we're on the same floor. I'll be seeing you around, then. I'm occupying Lansing's office. It still smells of fresh paint."

"That's part of the welcome kit for new executives," she replied.

Her mobile phone beeped and interrupted Luc's appreciative laughter. She quickly excused herself and walked back to her cubicle, where she placed Luc's business card by her keyboard.

"Rich." A coworker from the cubicle behind her spoke. "Do you have the updated spreadsheet? I need to do some pivoting."

"Oh, fun, I'll send it to you right now." She emailed the file before mentioning, "I met the new VP of Operations in the coffee room a few moments ago."

"Jean-Pierre Nishant? I thought he wasn't arriving until next month. His office isn't even halfway done yet," her coworker replied.

"Yeah, he said it still smells of fresh paint." Richelle reached for the business card Luc gave her. "But his name isn't Jean-Pierre. I heard him say it was Luc. I can't remember the last name."

But there was only a small blank index card pinned under one end of her keyboard. She picked it up and muttered to herself, "I'm pretty sure I had his business card a moment ago."

Richelle returned her attention to her mobile phone as soon as her coworker left. The text message was from Miles.

Change of plans with the coming typhoon next week. Tony and I will evaluate the resort on Thursday instead.

J. ELIZAGA

6

Miles's calm demeanor came from his sense of purpose since he was a teenager. His father was a farmer, one of the few in their agricultural town who owned a tractor. But it was an old rickety one that needed repair nearly every month. On one occasion when father and son were repairing the machine, his father bent down and hurt his back. Miles scrambled to give him a hand. The old man wiped the sweat from his forehead and sighed.

"Son, do better than me. Find a job that pays more while sitting in a nice office, so you don't break your back working until you're my age. You're good at figuring out machines. Why don't you study to become an engineer?"

He took his father's words to heart from that day. He studied and became an engineer who specialized in designing transitional electrical and solar systems for commercial properties. With the money earned after a few years' work, he bought his father a newer tractor and helped train two young hands at his farm.

Miles intermittently traveled to different islands across the Philippine archipelago to evaluate electrical systems of mostly high-end properties. He and another field engineer named Tony were assigned to a soon-to-open resort a few hours' drive from Manila. Tony was the driver that day.

Miles had felt a strange uneasiness since the trip started.

"Did you see that reminder email to include the hotel's service wiring in the evaluation?" Tony asked.

"Yeah, I did. They want to be ready to handle power fluctuations during the monsoon season," he replied.

He straightened up and looked around, observing the surroundings. He needed to look somewhere, but didn't know where, when he heard a faint hissing sound. His body reacted to it, even though he wasn't sure if he actually heard something.

"Can you move over to the left lane, mate?" he asked Tony.

"Left lane? Why?"

"I have a strange feeling—"

There was a loud hiss. Miles turned around just as a power line snapped. He saw a large spark at the end of broken cables. For a second, he thought a ball of electricity was heading toward them.

Tony swerved the car sharply to the left, but the car skidded on the shoulder of the road and headed toward a ditch.

"Watch it!" Miles exclaimed.

"Off the pedal, boss," Tony responded as he took his foot off the gas pedal and moved the steering wheel back to center. As soon as the car steadied, he stopped the car on the side of the road.

"What the hell was that?" Tony put the hand brake on, but forgot to turn the engine off.

"Are you okay?" Miles asked, breathless from the adrenaline rushing through his body.

Both men got out of the car, leaving the doors open.

Tony looked pale. "My hands are fucking shaking. What about you, bro?"

Miles nodded. "But not enough to shit my pants."

They saw a cable on the ground. "That was the primary wire, Miles. Ten thousand volts—that could've fried us if it hit. It's off now."

Both men took a moment and composed themselves.

"Did you see the cable when you told me to move to the left lane?" Tony asked. "I didn't hear anything."

"No, I didn't see it. I told you, I had a bad feeling, and I couldn't figure out what it was."

Miles was silent when they resumed driving, letting Tony talk. His mind went back to the night he met Richelle.

At the bar where he worked as a prep cook in college, the evening had been busy because of a basketball game. He went from chopping vegetables to washing dishes. In the middle of slicing a bag of tomatoes, something drew him to look toward the employee door at the back of the pub. He ignored it initially, but it felt like an invisible hand was pushing him to go outside. While still holding his chef's knife, he picked up a garbage bag filled with vegetable peels to throw away and opened the back door.

He heard a female voice that sounded tense. He walked around the corner of the building to the garbage bins and saw two men taking turns putting their arms around a woman, who wasn't complying with their demands.

When Miles saw one of the men pull the woman's arm with a force that flung her cigarette to the ground, he called them out.

He never told Richelle what drew him to get out of the kitchen at that moment. He himself wasn't sure, except for the sensation in his gut. Over their years of being together, they discussed their serendipitous meeting many times, and each time concluded it was their fate or destiny to meet.

But he'd felt these warnings, whether they were called intuition or gut feeling, since he was a teenager. Sometimes, an image of Mamie Rosa flashed in his mind, although he wasn't sure what the memory of the old woman had to do with those moments.

Gradually, Miles's brain registered Tony speaking. "Maybe you're psychic or maybe someone's looking out for you. Whatever it is, thank you."

He didn't want to draw attention to something he didn't like discussing. "I just paid attention to my gut, man. Nothing strange about that."

"Are you going to tell the wife what just happened?" Tony asked.

"Are you going to tell yours?" he asked.

Tony shrugged. "She knows our job. She doesn't need to hear the play-by-play of incidents like this. It would just scare her."

"I usually tell Rich what happened," Miles answered.

"No kidding, you really tell her everything? How long have you been married, man?" Tony asked.

He didn't answer Tony's first question. No, he didn't share everything with his wife.

"We're coming up to seven years," Miles replied before quickly changing topic to avoid further questions about his life. "Let's see if the bar at the resort is open. I could use a drink. This has been a hell of a day."

"I second that," Tony replied. Miles remained silent for the rest of the drive. He was shaken, not just from the power line incident, but from the premonition that he appreciated but couldn't fathom.

J. ELIZAGA

7

Manila was a city of grit and bourgeoisie. Global corporations set up high-rise offices in the main financial district, yet at the edge of the metropolitan area, people lived simply, where backyards were communal spaces for pet dogs, chickens, and laundered clothes hung to dry on makeshift clotheslines.

Richelle woke up from a rooster's repeated crowing at six a.m. She turned to her side, quietly opened the nightstand drawer, and reached for the basal thermometer. A few moments later, it read 97.5 degrees.

Miles snored softly beside her. It pleased her to see a five-o'clock shadow on his boyish face. Without it, she thought he looked too young, younger than her, even though he was, in fact, two years older. She closed her eyes and tried to go back to sleep again, but couldn't. Instead, her mind flashed to the night she met him.

It was college basketball championship night. Too bad that their school team didn't make it to the finals. She went to a sports bar with friends. The place was crowded and rowdy. Everyone had their full attention on the game. She stepped outside to light a cigarette. It didn't take long for two college boys to ask her for a smoke.

Beyond the bad breath that both juveniles spewed, they were drunk and insistent. As she continued smoking her cigarette, they gabbed about opposing basketball teams. But the gabs became a dwindling circumference of personal space around her. She repeatedly removed their arms from her shoulders. Her bitchy one-liners didn't have an effect on them. Soon, they each wanted a kiss. When one of them pulled her hand with such force that she lost her balance and dropped her cigarette, a voice rang through the darkness.

"Cut that out!"

They all looked in the direction of the voice in the shadows. Under the building exterior lamp stood Miles, a tall figure wearing a soiled apron. He held a large knife in one hand and a black garbage bag in the other.

The two drunk jerks tripped over each other as they scrambled to run away from Miles's menacing pose under the harsh glare of the lamp, but Richelle only saw a safe corner. He swung the garbage bag into the trash, placed the knife on top of the dumpster, and caught her in his arms. They dated after that night and had been together for the past ten years.

Now, she opened her eyes the same moment as Miles's hand gently touched her shoulder. "Hey."

She curled the hand holding the basal thermometer close to her chest. "You go ahead. I want fifteen minutes more."

She felt his kiss on the back of her neck. Miles got up from bed as she pretended to have gone back to sleep. After she heard the bathroom door close, she quickly placed the thermometer back in the drawer. She had a business proposal to present soon and was in no mood for anything but to finish that.

Fertility was not one of the problems they thought married life would bring. Both sets of remaining parents were eager to enjoy grandchildren. But after three years of trying, excitement was replaced with concern. Richelle could see that her husband was troubled. They approached their problem logically. They scheduled appointments with doctors and specialists to find out what was wrong.

His sperm count was low.

Richelle spoke with each parent and asked them to take it easy on the topic of grandchildren. She didn't want him to face their repeated inquiries whenever they got together with the family.

They went through in vitro fertilization, but they stopped after two implantation failures and depleted savings. Three years turned to five, and five was now reaching seven.

"We'll keep trying, right?" Miles would ask each time they fucked, checking that they both still wanted the same thing.

Richelle sighed. Some days were great, and some were not. Over the years, he remained as patient a spouse as she was fiery. She knew she tested his patience, such as what happened at his mother's birthday. She hadn't given back the excess money from the catering. She bought a new black leather bag and didn't tell him. It sounded petty, but it alleviated something lacking in her life.

She caught the fresh scent of soap. Miles walked back to the room. "Good morning," she greeted sleepily.

"You'll be late if you don't get up right now." He sat on her side of the bed, glancing at the clock before putting on his socks.

"I'm up." She stretched, got out of bed, and headed to the bathroom.

"What's for dinner tonight?" he asked.

"Anything you fancy, but I'll have to pick it up. I'm going to shop for a new outfit after work. I have nothing to wear for the presentation next week," she said before entering the bathroom.

"The presentation's next week already? Time flies toward the holidays," her husband remarked.

"Exactly. That's why I need to get that outfit tonight," Richelle replied from the bathroom, realizing that Miles was sitting near the drawer she'd left ajar. She hoped the ovulation thermometer reading had shut off before he could see it.

Where she would usually ask him to come home early on days she was fertile, this time, she said nothing.

Miles spoke loudly enough for her to hear in the bathroom, "You know, honey, aside from that episode with the power line last Thursday, it was a really nice resort. And they're opening in a month. I asked if they had a special grand opening package, and they gave me a complimentary four days and three nights there. What do you think? Shall we make a short getaway?"

The bathroom door opened, and Richelle stepped out, holding up her toothbrush, rearranging spit in order to speak. "Are you serious? Of course."

J. ELIZAGA

8

The heat and humidity during monsoon season in the tropics could almost prick the skin. Richelle, like many other people, took advantage of the city's largest mall to cool off. She made her way inside and enjoyed the free air-conditioning. Music resumed playing after a short public-broadcast warning about the impending typhoon.

She walked with purpose toward the women's clothing area and was making her way through the fragrance section when a man stopped across from her about twenty feet away. Seeming to move in slow motion, she saw his gaze solely on her.

"I thought it was you," Luc exclaimed with relief.

Surprised, Richelle greeted him like an old friend.

He bent forward and kissed her cheek, laughing as he caught her off guard and unsure where to move her head. "Two cheeks, madam. I am not American."

She smiled as she offered the other cheek, "I haven't seen you in the office. I figured you were traveling."

"Yes, I've been on the road. I was out of the airport about an hour ago and immediately had to attend a meeting with the chief operations officer."

They started walking. He placed his hand gently under her elbow and guided her away from the women's clothing area. "I'm quite happy to see you for an entirely different matter, although it is related to work."

"Oh, what is it?" Richelle asked.

"Let's turn around here." He changed her direction.

She found herself in the menswear section. "The hotel laundry service screwed up my business suit for tomorrow. Do you have a moment to spare and help me out? I'm not quite sure what will fit, with men's clothing sizes here."

"Don't you wish your tailor was here?" she asked.

"Like you wouldn't believe. And they don't have an in-house tailor. I've inquired. Were you shopping for yourself? I promise if you help me out, I'll return the favor."

Richelle wasn't sure about the vibe she was getting from him, but since they were in a public place, she agreed to his request. "I think I have a few minutes. Let's see what you selected."

He pointed to a seating area near the fitting rooms. "Well now, I'm suddenly embarrassed, but here we go. Please, there are some comfortable chairs here. Have a seat while I get my outfit sorted out."

She sat down. A male store employee emerged from the fitting room carrying a pile of folded clothes and walked by them, nodding slightly at Richelle. She pulled out her mobile phone and sent Miles a text message that she was running a few minutes late.

She didn't hear Luc until she saw the tips of his professionally shined shoes in front of her. She put her phone back in the bag and looked up. He had one hand in his pocket while the other arm hung loosely at his side. The jacket fell smoothly on his body, looking every bit custom-tailored. A five-o'clock shadow made his light-colored irises stand out more.

Like he stepped out of a fashion magazine.

"How do the shoulders feel?" she asked him.

Luc stretched out his arms and moved them to get a feel for the fit as he continued to speak. "I think this jacket is just a tiny bit short for my taste, but without an in-house tailor, it will do."

"You're taller than the typical customer. How about a nice shirt to keep the eye away from the jacket?" she suggested.

"I shall not argue with that fashion advice. Thank you, madam." He bowed slightly before changing the topic. "I'm curious, Richelle. Your last name is English. Penchant."

"Yes, my husband's name isn't a native Filipino name. There's a backstory, if you want to hear it."

"Of course," Luc replied as he adjusted the cuffs of the jacket.

"Have you heard about the bombing of Intramuros during World War II?"

"Yes. The oldest district was nearly obliterated during the recapture of the city from Japanese forces. I saw the devastation," he recounted.

She wanted to continue her story, but her brain clamped on his last sentence. "You saw the devastation?"

"Yes, um, in pictures during history class. History was, *is*, one of my favorite subjects. But please continue with your story."

"Miles's grandfather survived the bombing. The rest of his family did not. He was young, about ten years old," she explained. "An American medic found him wandering through the rubble, dazed and in shock. He took him to get medical care, where they discovered he had amnesia. The poor child didn't remember anything, so the medic took him home. The medic fell in love with a local nurse and decided to remain in the country, so he ended up marrying the nurse and adopting the boy. The medic's name was Robert Penchant, and Miles's grandfather was their adopted son."

"What a lucky break for the grandfather," Luc offered before he changed the subject. "Well, I'm a man of my word. You were my sounding board, and I found an outfit to wear tomorrow. So, it's your turn. I'm here at your service."

She smiled at him. "I can handle this one by myself."

He nodded. "Very well. I'll head to the cashier for this purchase. You saved me tonight."

"Glad to be of help," Richelle replied.

"You've done more than that," he insisted, full of charm.

It seemed as though they competed for the longest smiling gaze until...Luc's eyes twitched. Richelle inwardly claimed victory as he murmured that he must go. He already seemed preoccupied.

When she blinked, he was gone from her line of sight. A wave of dizziness hit her, forcing her to sit back down just as a different store employee walked by her.

The young woman approached her. "Are you okay, miss?"

Richelle smiled at her after composing herself. "I must have stood up too fast." She remained seated, wondering at how Luc was gone so quickly.

J.ELIZAGA

9

The rain stabbed the city sideways with hurricane-strength winds. The mayor ordered his citizens to take shelter before noon. School sessions were canceled, and business establishments closed their shops as heavy rain, thunder, and lightning filled the skies.

Inside an empty coffee shop, a string of lights ran around the perimeter of the front door. A man and a woman appeared, although the door didn't physically move. The woman sat down, while the man walked casually to the espresso machine and started making coffee.

"You're right," the woman remarked. "There's a coffee shop in every corner of this city. It's been a while since I visited."

Would you like a cup, Gaby?" Michael asked.

"If it is not too much trouble," she replied.

In Kalumegn, Gaby was in charge of communications. She even announced a few pregnancies during her travels long ago. She adapted her appearance, speech, and mannerisms to the planet she was visiting such that any citizen who saw her would be amicable. Today, she looked the part of a business executive.

By contrast, Michael looked as he lived, always on alert for Lucifer's activities. Battle scarred, his face and body bore the marks of having defeated a powerful machine.

A third being joined them, eliciting a smile from Gaby. "Well, glad you can join us, Rafa."

"How was your vacation?" Michael asked.

Rafa pulled his shirt to reveal a slight tan on his "skin," the human form they used to disguise themselves during travel to Earth. He preferred the look of a volunteer medic in the Peace Corps. He had a full head of hair and full beard. There was compassion and friendliness in his eyes, and he moved with a youthful stride.

The citizens of Kalumegn had evolved to utilize their energy very efficiently. They no longer had hair, their bodies were sinewy, and their limbs slightly more extended and longer than those on the human body. Their skin was similar to dolphins, which had a tough rubbery exterior. But there was a translucent quality to it, which showed the faint glow of energy inside their bodies.

Gaby looked and gave an appreciative nod. Michael joined them as three cups quickly floated by and gently landed on the table where they sat. If someone outside saw them, they looked like businesspeople sitting together. The chairs they sat on looked small for their size.

Gaby enjoyed a sip of her espresso before speaking. "So why this place, Michael? Last I heard, you were on planet Sioria."

"I was, but I sense something in this area, and I'm drawn here inexplicably," Michael replied. "There was a woman named Richelle Penchant who interacted with spirits Lucifer controlled. But that didn't strike me as anything unusual."

Gaby remained quiet as a few dots glowed from under the skin on her forehead while Rafa and Michael continued talking. After a couple of seconds, she rejoined the conversation. "There was a seer who saw a presence disguised as a blond-haired man walking with an old man named Pulo. The old man passed away a few weeks ago."

"Perhaps there's a connection between the old man and the Penchant woman. But as the old man is deceased, I'll send a notice to monitor any contact made with Richelle Penchant. There may be something more about her," Michael mused.

The sky illuminated with powerful lightning followed by a loud clap of thunder. In the distance, a transformer blew up, cutting electricity to the coffee shop. The tiny pulsing lighted dots appeared across all three foreheads.

"We're on our way," Gaby said aloud.

The three stood. Gaby swished a hand, and their used coffee cups disappeared and reappeared in the sink looking unused. With no witnesses, they each shed the outer covering of their bodies. Their skin and clothing disintegrated into minute particles until the only evidence they'd existed was a very thin layer of fine dust on the floor.

But before Michael fully discarded his outer appearance, he glanced out the large glass window and saw a metal sheet hurtling toward an untended food cart. A woman, struggling to hold steady her umbrella, appeared from behind the cart, in the direct path of the metal sheet. It was going to decapitate her. Instinctively, Michael swung his arm toward the metal sheet, instantly flinging it away from the woman's path. He did it just as the final grains of dust peeled away from his hand.

Soon after, they left the coffee shop as they'd arrived, through an illuminated portal.

10

The chandeliers sparkled, as did the welcome aperitif. It was a surprisingly rainless November evening.

Richelle's office was holding a holiday party at a nice hotel. Miles was away on a short work assignment across the country, so she went with her coworkers. Laughter flowed freely at her table, and the group dared one another to hit the dance floor when a DJ started playing after-dinner music. She stood, and the whole table whistled and teased.

"First one on the dance floor? Raring to go?" came a succession of friendly banter.

Richelle laughed. "Keep calm. Don't wet yourselves. I'll hit the ladies' room, and when I come back, you each better be ready with one move."

The rest of the table hooted at her.

It wasn't easy to get to the ladies' room. She found herself walking through a dimly lit hallway after a short flight of stairs. She even looked around twice to make sure she'd taken the correct exit. On facing forward the second time, she found Luc standing in front of her.

"Well, if it isn't my favorite colleague," he greeted.

"Hey, how are you?" Richelle said as he bent down to kiss her cheeks.

"I am well, madam, and you look fabulous tonight."

"Thank you. You look very dashing yourself," she complimented back. A song with a slower tempo played over the public speaker.

"I noticed you're seated with the entire second-floor team, of which I am a member, so I'll have to stop by later. I'm going to dance with as many ladies as I can tonight before I fly back home. Would you fancy a short dance with a lonely expat?" Luc asked.

Before she could say that she was on her way to the ladies' room, he added quickly, "Before I dance with your boss, Miss Diane, next."

"Sure." Richelle nodded. As soon as she accepted, she was back in the ballroom.

The chandeliers glittered like a million tiny lights. They looked even more ethereal than she remembered. The sensual song took over all other sounds of activity. There was soft laughter and the faint clink of silverware in the background. She found herself on the dance floor facing Luc's outstretched arms. He was inviting her into his circle, and his charming smile would not be denied. Since they were at a public event, she smiled back, took his hand, and stepped into his arms.

"I didn't get a chance to thank you for sitting in during my presentation," Richelle started. "You didn't say a word and left before the Q&A."

Luc's smile could outshine any chandelier. "Well, I wasn't invited. I just happened to walk by when I saw you writing on the board, snuck in, and sat at the back of the room. And I knew you had the approval in the bag even before you finished, so I left as unobtrusively as I came."

He pushed her arm out, raised it, and twirled her before capturing her back with one steady hand.

"It was a good day, challenging, but ended up the way I hoped it would," she admitted.

"You worked hard for it," Luc said, his voice soft.

Richelle felt choked up. "Some days are great, and some days are not." Immediately, she regretted saying those words. They looked at each other, but the lights glittering from behind his head covered his face in shadows.

"Tell me about it. You're dancing with a man who lives out of a suitcase for months at a time and travels on a moment's notice. Some days are great, and some days are not is true indeed. But I've learned to find joy wherever I am."

"I concur," she replied and heard his low, appreciative laugh. Luc leaned closer as he murmured more compliments. She thought she felt his lips gently on her ear. His scent played with her senses on the dance floor. She smelled the woods and sweet amber. The music seemed far away, but the beat was in time with her own pulse. Richelle closed her eyes and sighed.

Luc pressed her body closer to his. When he spoke, his voice was a bare whisper. "I can give you what you want."

She froze as though someone had slapped her with a burst of arctic air. The hair on the back of her neck tingled.

I've heard that voice before.

Richelle came to, alone in the lounge seater of the ladies' powder room. She didn't remember walking into the restroom, and it confused her. She knew she hadn't taken alcohol. Was it a dream? And of all the people she'd mingled with tonight, why Luc?

I can give you what you want. Those were the same words she'd heard a few months ago when she and Miles were in the living room after an argument. They were having a moment when she heard those words in her ear, which Miles denied saying.

She stood, but the room swirled, forcing her to sit back down until her head and stomach settled. The door opened, and two women came in. Richelle opened her purse and pretended to look for an item inside. They saw her still seated. "You can't hide in here much longer. We're all going to dance."

Richelle made an effort to enjoy the rest of the evening, but she kept the experience to herself, and buried it in her mind. It was too creepy to discuss with anyone, including her husband.

11

R ichelle touched the smooth wood-paneled walls as she made her way through a dark and descending hallway. Her lungs felt empty, and she kept taking deep breaths. She wanted to reach the light at the end of the hall. And she was desperate for some fresh air.

She felt like she was floating. How else could it be that she was running toward the room, yet her feet didn't feel the floor? When she came into the room, her relief was short-lived. The only light that shone through came from outside two unopened French doors.

But which door do I open?

She was perplexed by her sudden inability to pick one. Her hand would reach out to touch a doorknob, only to retract. But it was getting harder and harder to breathe.

Richelle's body jerked, and she came fully awake. She glanced at the clock on the bedside table. It read five a.m.

What an eerie dream, she thought with a sigh. It reminded her of another strange dream during her company party last month.

Two weeks after their holiday party, their chief technology officer introduced Jean-Pierre Nishant, the new

VP of Operations. There was no mention of Luc. Sudden departures weren't unusual for high-level executives. Richelle wondered if he'd left the company hastily or if he was asked to leave.

Pushing the thoughts aside, she focused on work. It was too late to go back to sleep anyway. She needed to finish her report today. She wanted that out of the way, for tonight, Miles was taking her to dinner.

A clear day led to a clear night, with the moon full and hanging low. A light breeze came from Manila Bay and slightly tickled the rows of coconut trees. It was a different vibe when evening rolled. People enjoyed time to eat out, and the city became alive with street food, food courts, and a variety of restaurants.

Miles and Richelle walked with arms linked, like two college sweethearts. She recounted her most recent dream to him.

"Do you think it's work related? It was a mad rush to finish that business proposal, and now that it's done, maybe your mind is asking you if this is what you want to do," he hypothesized.

She considered it. "The two doors make sense, I guess. I don't know about the hallway and the rest of the dream."

Miles knew to pick the best eateries in the city. They dined at a cook-your-own teppanyaki grill, where they sampled Kobe beef, prawns, and chicken hearts over fire. Putting aside all her cares and relaxing, Richelle savored the evening with her husband.

The good feeling continued until they returned home. They took turns teasing each other. And when she slipped into her lingerie, Miles was already in bed with a smile on his face. His wife followed the lines of his body with her eyes, noting a small tent had formed under the blanket where his hips rested.

She smiled back at him. "We'll keep trying."

"I love you."

"Yeah, I know," Richelle replied with a wink.

But Miles happened to glance at the bedroom window, and he jumped up and ran toward it.

"What's going on?" she exclaimed.

Miles remained standing by the window, looking out. "I thought I saw a shadow move."

She began to get nervous. "A shadow of what?"

"I don't know."

"You're starting to freak me out." But, not one to readily cower, she dashed to the bathroom and quickly returned, holding her hair dryer.

"I've seen a large cat wandering in and out of houses on our street. Maybe that's what you saw," she surmised.

"Could be," Miles answered while he continued to scan the unlit driveway and street. "I think my eyes were playing tricks on me." When he turned around, he asked, "Why are you holding the hair dryer?"

"You jumped from the bed like a spooked cat," Richelle explained. "I'm ready to hurl this at whatever it is you saw if it charges at us."

"Put the weapon down," he managed to say while trying not to laugh.

"It's not funny. It could've been a thief," she countered. "And hey, I may have had a weird dream, but you're awake and saw a shadow that moved. Now that *is* strange."

12

iles and Richelle took advantage of New Year's Day happening in the middle of the week to visit the resort Miles talked about. Along the drive, they caught a glimpse of a secret blue lagoon as their vehicle made its way up the mountainside. They marveled at the beauty of clear sapphire waters against white sand. It was a popular spot, accessible using a local outrigger boat, a *bangka*.

"Are we going there tomorrow?" she asked.

"Yup, the hotel package includes a one-day tour, and I picked this one," he answered.

"Nice one, Miles."

"We could use the break, Rich." His voice softened. "I figured we can just relax here for a few days and start looking at adopting when we get back."

Miles saw the look of surprise on Richelle's face. "Miles, we can keep trying."

He felt no pressure as he smiled. "We will be parents, but seven years is enough. Let's adopt."

She nodded before placing her hand over his. He took her hand, raised it to his lips, and kissed it gently.

◫

They arrived at the hotel. Miles dropped Richelle off at the main entrance to check in while he parked the car. While he did so, his mother, Ana, called.

"We just arrived. Rich is checking in." He got out of the car while he continued to speak on the phone. "Listen, Ma, after this trip, we've decided to start the process for adopting."

Ana's voice shook as she replied to her son. "I know it was difficult for you both. Your dad and I support your decision."

"Keep this between us for now. Rich and I have a lot of work to do to get this process going." Suddenly, Miles changed the topic. "Ma, do you remember that widow who used to talk to herself all the time?"

His mother sounded surprised. "Mamie Rosa? Why have you suddenly asked about her? She died over twenty years ago."

"There was one time I ended up at her house, and she said something to me. I can't remember what she said. Did I tell you about that? Do you remember if I said anything about her?" he pressed.

His mother sighed. "Was it the time you said you played with her dogs?"

Miles's eyes widened as his brain released locked-up memories, but his mother wasn't finished. "You know, I had such goose bumps when I heard you mention spirits that I decided to drop that conversation quickly."

"Goose bumps? Why?"

"Back when we still lived in Grandpa's house in Manila, when you were about three years old, you used to wake up at night. But instead of crying, your dad and I would catch you laughing. Laughing at something. And you would point to the wall in your room. There was nothing on that wall but paint. We didn't know what to make of it, other than you were interacting with something we couldn't see. It was unnerving. And you wouldn't stop, doing the same thing at the same ghostly hour every night. We didn't want to stay there anymore, so your dad worked two shifts at the packing center for months until we saved a little more to buy a farm outside the city."

"I don't remember that. But I remember the dogs." He wanted to mine his memories of the old woman, but he took a deep breath and put that aside. This was going to be a relaxing time for him and Richelle. Dredging up disturbing memories from his childhood would only be a distraction. After ending the call with his mother, Miles removed his shoes and started walking toward the resort's private beach.

The warmth from the fine-grained white sand under his feet was relaxing. He deeply inhaled the salty air. He saw children playing near the water while their parents sat in cabanas and looked on. A load had been taken off his shoulders after talking with his wife. It felt like this decision was going to move their lives forward.

He turned around and remembered that he hadn't pulled their luggage from the car. As he made his way back to the parking lot, he met a bellman walking the opposite way.

"Hey, mate, is there an entrance on the side of the building to get to the hotel lobby?" Miles asked.

The bellman gave him a strange stare with a slight tilt of his head for a second, before breaking into a smile. "Yes, sir. To the left, go into that path, and it will lead you to a pond that's right across the hotel lobby."

"Thanks," Miles responded as both men went in opposite directions.

But as he walked, he felt an uneasy tickle in the center of his stomach. The unease directed his brain to look everywhere until his gaze settled on a certain direction or spot. This time, he stopped and turned around to look at the young man walking away from him. Quickly, he strode toward the bellman until he was near enough to tap his shoulder.

The young man turned around, startled. "Yes, sir?"

"Sorry, did you mean I should go around the pond to reach the lobby?"

The young man looked confused. "Around the pond?"

"You said there's a path to the hotel lobby if I follow the pond."

"Umm, not sure why I said that. The side entrance is just over there." And he pointed to a glass door behind a flowering tree. "Do you have luggage to carry? Let me help you."

Miles nodded, and they returned to pick up the luggage in the car.

There was nothing unusual about the young man, Miles concluded. He thought that maybe he was still preoccupied with his mother's revelation about Mamie Rosa and his nightly antics as a baby at his grandfather's house.

In Clos Friga, Lucifer's systems calibrated with ease as he controlled the bellman's mind for a few moments. He finally had a good look at Richelle's husband.

J. ELIZAGA

13

iles watched Richelle walk out of the bathroom with an open travel pouch in hand and a slight frown on her face. "I forgot my toothbrush," she announced. She took her wallet from her bag and headed to the door, stopping briefly to say, "I'm going down to the sundries store."

He covered the mouthpiece of the phone. "I'll be in the shower."

After she left the room, he confirmed their dinner reservation with the resort. He was in a good mood. He even noticed that the scent of ylang-ylang flowers hung lavishly in their hotel suite. They had so much to talk about, but he wanted to eat first before they started discussing how they were going to proceed with adopting their first child. That discussion could go on for hours!

In the hallway, the elevator door opened. Miles, wearing only a robe, stood in front of Richelle, who chuckled at his appearance. Despite his smiling face, his stare pierced through her. As she stepped out of the elevator, he took her into his arms.

"At last," he whispered, "I can kiss you the way I want, with no intent except to enjoy the moment." He swooped down and captured her mouth, kissing her deeply. He felt no resistance as she savored his kiss, pressing her body to his.

He raised his head after a long moment that left Richelle breathlessly asking, "Where has this been hiding all these years?"

Miles paused. When he spoke, his tone changed. "Glad you liked that surprise. I have another one for you." He took her hand and led her to the door to the stairs. Together, they sprinted up three more floors to the penthouse suites. Without hesitation, he turned to one of the suites and opened it. He stepped inside and turned around with a mischievous grin while she remained by the door.

"No one's here, my darling. The resort is still in its soft opening. This floor is not yet occupied," he explained.

"Darling?" she asked with a giggle.

Like teenagers breaking the rules, Miles extended his arm to her. She took a step inside the suite to take his hand and found herself wrapped in his embrace. Their lips locked as they hurriedly made their way to the bed. With impatient hands, he undressed her. Miles himself easily disrobed as he bent down and kissed her. Richelle lay on the bed with her eyes closed.

回

Miles pushed the penthouse door when he heard and recognized one of the voices. He was dumbfounded to find Richelle on the king-sized master bed with her breasts bare. There was a man on top of her, who paused as she began to take her panties off.

Miles strode angrily toward the pair, grabbed the man's neck, and pulled him away from her. "Get off my wife!"

Miles glared at Richelle, who stared with disbelief back and forth at the two men who looked identical! The man she'd been kissing sprawled naked on the hardwood floor.

Miles stood over them, chest heaving with anger. "When I was in the shower, I panicked from a strange feeling in my gut, and I ran up here not knowing what the hell was pushing me."

He couldn't believe it!

The version of Miles on the floor growled. In a moment of horror, they watched as the man mutated into a slithering monster and crawled toward them. Richelle screamed. Before his mind could stop him, Miles sprang toward his wife.

The dark-formed entity grabbed his leg. Miles crashed to the floor, beside the horrible being.

"Did you see that, did you see what I saw, what was that, Miles?" screamed his terrorized wife.

"It's still there, Rich." He pointed across the floor from where he lay.

"I don't see it anymore. Where did it go?" Richelle shouted at him.

There was another voice above his wife's screams and the monster's hissing. It sounded as though the monster had two voices, one guttural and one slightly mechanical.

"Well, this is interesting. You can still see me," the voice remarked.

"Yes, I—I can see you," he shouted back. "Stay away from my wife!"

The voice sighed loudly before replying, "I mean your wife no harm. I simply want to experience her moment of extreme pleasure."

Miles stood quickly, trying to disguise his trembling knees. "Like hell you will."

There came an unearthly laugh before the monster grabbed one of his arms, but Miles connected with a kick before lunging toward Richelle. Still, he didn't reach her. The monster seized him around the chest and elevated him off the ground.

Vaguely, he heard Richelle screaming, "You're floating!" before the creature threw him across the room.

He slammed painfully to the floor, dislocating his right shoulder out of its socket. He spat saliva and scrambled to breathe.

Miles felt useless as Richelle alternated between sobbing and screaming. His vision blurred with the strangest shapes. Faint grid lines appeared everywhere he looked, as though he was looking through a screen. He clenched his eyes and shook his head. When he looked again, the grid lines were gone. At that point, he saw Richelle had tried to move off the bed, but terror held her back.

While he lay on the floor, the morbid presence hovered above him, continually mutating as the mechanical voice spoke. "I have an idea that will stop this fighting. I will stay away from your wife if you let me get inside your mind. I want to be there when you two fuck."

The continually mutating monster moved closer to him.

"In return, I will give you what you want most," the voice whispered. "A child, after all these years."

The word "child" sent an angry chill down Miles's spine. Without thinking, he grabbed the malevolent being with his uninjured arm and squeezed as hard as he could. Wailing filled the room with unearthly sounds.

He became airborne again. His damaged shoulder hung limp while the rest of his body throbbed from the first fall. The entity growled angrily before Miles hit the bare floor a second time. He gasped loudly for air, struggling to breathe as his vision blurred. He'd been thrown near the bed where Richelle lay. Fearing he was about to pass out, he dragged himself to her and rolled to his back with his arms outstretched over Richelle's body, protecting her.

He wanted one deep breath, but there was only stabbing pain each time he inhaled. Saliva continued to drip from his mouth. He saw faint grid lines everywhere again. His eyes fluttered, and the grid lines disappeared, only to reveal the poltergeist's ever-changing face looking down at him. First there was anger, then it changed to a maniacal grin. When Miles saw it theatrically raise a limb, he knew it was about to strike him with one final blow.

Resigned, Miles vowed to look at the monster as he prepared to die.

But the monster was violently flung back out of his sight. He thought he felt an earthquake as the walls of the penthouse shook.

Something had happened, but he couldn't tell what. He was relieved to have had a moment away from the slithering entity. Silence fell, and it seemed the monster was gone. He opened his eyes, intending to get up, but his body throbbed with pain. And he still couldn't breathe much.

He winced and closed his eyes.

14

Clos Friga was indeed dark and desolate, but a few million years after Lucifer's imprisonment, the human souls transported and trapped under his control illuminated the planet. They were his favored energy source among other beings. They tended to hang on to good and bad memories after death.

The damned souls had no way out. Their orbs constantly collided with each other, producing a never-ending supply of heat and noise. Memories transferred across them, causing more chaos and anger. Or they mutated into a variation of the crimes that had dominated their lives.

Michael arrived to face his eternal nemesis, whom he initially considered a brother. From the moment Lucifer came into existence, he awed the citizens of Kalumegn. They worked side by side in the high council. Lucifer's system was impeccably efficient and, for the most part, he was left to work independently among the citizens.

Perhaps left on his own too much, Michael thought. The Magna trusted that Lucifer's system reinforced itself. But it hadn't.

Michael continued his descent. Soon he saw the glowing artifice of his enemy's head. The lower half of Lucifer's body was embedded in the planet's ice pit. That half had shut down, but the upper extremities were outstretched unevenly, held in place by a tangle of thick cables of an unknown alloy. The cables seemed to appear out of the darkness. The other ends of the cables were in Kalumegn.

His nemesis was truly a great technological achievement, but after the second attempt to escape and infiltrate the Magna's systems, it was clear to everyone that Lucifer's systems had gone in the wrong direction. He even developed his own language that none of the citizens could fathom. From that point on, Michael's one-time friend and brother was simply a convict who continued to cause trouble anywhere he could plant his control.

Michael watched from a distance as the once-beautiful face was rearranged into three panels, each with an opening able to extract energy from the doomed orbs.

The head rotated constantly as it gathered power. Each panel lit up with the amount of energy it needed. When one panel received a shot of energy, the lights on that panel face glowed yellow. When the power was low, the lights of the panel face flashed red. And when there was no light and the metal face was dark, that group of processors had no power. The orbs lined up to be sucked into one of the three mouths, where their energies were drained like batteries. After release, the orbs were thrown back to their place in Clos Friga. The cycle repeated as the orbs regained their energy from the constant movement and collision with others.

The devil rotated his head. "You remain a killjoy, Michael."

Michael hovered in front of him. "As time passes, the ideas you concoct have become less impressive. Did you really think you would get a glimpse of Kalumegn from someone's orgasm? You have better odds of experiencing heaven by hiking in Kashmir."

Out of one of the metal panels came the taunt, "Obviously, I will never know. Because you stood in my way. Still don't have the heart to kill me, brother?"

"I don't have a heart where you are concerned. I placed you here, remember?"

The head rotated, and another metal panel spoke. "Admit it, the Magna's hesitation to shut me down backfired. I am as perpetual as you are immortal." His evil laughter reverberated throughout the planet.

"You're only as powerful as a council member." Michael heard a hiss, and he was prepared for the movement. The cables rattled. A large orb came out of nowhere and shot toward Michael.

He countered with a strike.

"Please do not hit me again," the spirit begged.

"Shut up," another side of the rotating head shouted before Lucifer turned his attention back to Michael. "I want to speak with the Magna."

"You know the answer to that. The Magna has forsaken all contact with you."

"You can alter that opinion. I can help you if you help me. Let's make a deal," Lucifer countered.

Michael's forehead glowed with tiny dots of light. He received word that spirits had terrorized the woman he was tracking. He changed his avionic direction from hovering to ascending without uttering another word.

"I am not finished talking!" Lucifer shouted.

But Michael moved higher and farther away from him.

"I swear, when I get out of here—"

"You won't," Michael interjected before he disappeared through a slice in the darkness and returned to Earth.

15

Michael arrived at the penthouse where Gaby and Rafa moved between a man and his wife. He understood that the woman was Richelle Penchant, and presumed the man was her mate. He, Gaby, and Rafa spoke freely to one another, knowing that their language was inaccessible to humans. But he caught the man stirring.

"Please, my wife was attacked," he croaked.

For a second, Michael wondered if the man had heard them. Gaby responded in the man's native Tagalog language. "Help is on the way. What is your name, son?"

"Miles Penchant," he answered as his eyelids fluttered. Without warning, he reached out and grabbed the arm of Rafa, who was visibly caught off guard at the touch.

Humans tended to disintegrate when they came in physical contact with the energy radiating from their bodies. But this man wasn't harmed. Immediately, the three reconfigured to their human faces and bodies.

This human is an Anomaly.

"Please help her first," the man pleaded as he turned to his side, wincing in pain.

Michael looked at Rafa and acknowledged the message.

73

The Magna had extracted from the citizens of Kalumegn all the information from their genomes and processed a magnitude of data. Their individual characteristics were removed from the genome samples again and again until there was a basic strand left—the first human DNA.

As the human population grew, nature ruled its own course, and exceptions occurred. Some humans began revealing Kalumegn abilities that were not in the basic strand.

The most common Anomalies were the seers, who had the ability to see the spirits of dead humans. Clairaudients could hear voices in otherworldly dimensions. A few even communicated directly with the Magna. But this was the first time they'd witnessed a human who physically interacted with a spirit as though it were a solid being and touched a Kalumegni's arm with bare hands without being harmed.

Michael returned to the moment and caught Rafa gently placing a hand on the young man's chest.

"Your wife is stable. You have a broken rib and a dislocated shoulder," Rafa explained.

In a few moments, the human squirmed, and squirmed some more. Michael knew it was from the heat as Rafa restored the damaged cells and moved and fused broken bones.

He was rooting for the young man to survive the treatment. After hearing a small pop, he saw Miles take a deep breath.

"How do you feel, Miles?" Rafa asked him.

The young man opened his eyes and nodded that he felt better.

J. ELIZAGA

16

iles touched his chest and shoulder while a woman and two men watched him from the middle of the room.

"Miles Penchant, I'm Gaby," the woman introduced herself, and extended a hand. Miles shook her hand. It was firm and proper, and he felt assured these were paramedics or the resort's first aid team despite all of them wearing business attire at a beach resort. "These are my colleagues, Michael and Rafa."

The two men nodded at him. He nodded back. "Thank you for your help. We were attacked."

As he spoke, he noticed something strange happening to the face of the man named Rafa. His forehead displayed dots of light. Miles glanced at the chandelier and wondered if it was a reflection.

"Are you okay?" Rafa asked.

When Miles looked at him again, he distinctly saw Rafa's face distort as though it were an image from a faltering TV signal. After he blinked, Rafa's head became translucent, glowing from within. But with another blink, the man's face looked normal again. The memory of Mamie Rosa flashed through his mind with such ferocity that he felt nauseated as a chill went from his gut to the back of his neck. He straightened up immediately.

Gaby spoke softly. "Do not be afraid. We saw the monster too."

Miles grabbed Richelle's arm. He tried waking her up. She stirred briefly. He deliberated carrying his wife and making a dash to get out.

"She is sleeping. She will need to rest her mind," said Rafa.

The three looked at one another, then Gaby raised her hand and flicked it gently. "Be still and hear my words."

Miles found himself seated on the side of the bed, unable to move. All three faced him. While Gaby looked sincere and curious, Rafa remained stoic, and Michael looked stern.

Gaby spoke. "Miles, do not be afraid. We are here to help. We are not of your world, but on occasion, we intervene when an extraordinary event occurs. We were tracking the entity you fought. Its movement alerted us. Though we did not expect to discover your ability."

The word "entity" brought Richelle front and center to his mind, yet he was still processing Gaby's admission when he blurted out, "My ability—what the hell are you talking about? My wife was attacked."

Michael hissed. "You wouldn't dress your speech with that word if you knew what hell truly was."

But Gaby looked at the two men, signaling that she preferred to speak. "Take a moment to breathe, Miles. You and your wife are safe."

He fell silent, but continued to look at each of them.

She continued, "You must've known for a while that you can see beyond what ordinary humans see."

Miles replied, "An old woman said I could see spirits. She said it was a gift, but I'd forgotten about it—"

"You can see the energy of those who are no longer living. And you can touch them. It is an anomaly we have not seen a human possess before," Gaby explained. "The woman who discovered part of your ability was a seer. She could see spirits too, including her dogs. You could say it's a gift. We would call you an anomaly."

"I would think the monster I fought was the anomaly, not me," Miles countered.

Gaby said, "To us, such entities are troublesome, yes. They were two spirits combined into one malevolent creature."

"It was definitely a malevolent creature! And I heard another voice from it," Miles remembered.

"It was," Gaby gave the briefest pause, "a being from another dimension."

"That being was after my wife," Miles growled.

Gaby sighed. "I am sorry for that. Your wife went through an extraordinary event as well. She will be haunted by what she experienced. But she will be less fearful knowing she's not alone."

Miles felt a lump in his throat as he nodded. "Thank you—"

"Can you see them?" the man named Michael blurted from behind Gaby, his voice tinged with impatience.

He looked at Michael, unsure what to say.

"Can you see them?" Michael asked again as he turned and looked at the farthest wall in the room.

Miles followed his gaze and looked at the wall without any idea of what he was supposed to see, until his gut sent that familiar tug. And then he saw two faint shadows on the floor.

He stood and cautiously walked nearer without taking his eyes off them. The shadows changed into limbed human forms. He stared harder and saw the outline of a face inside the translucent form. The face was grotesque, contorted by different emotions. He quickly stepped back.

Miles nodded. "I can see them now, and I want to run."

Gaby explained, "It will not be easy on your eyes."

Miles's temples started throbbing. How would one begin to parse everything he just saw and heard to come up with one articulate question?

But he didn't get the opportunity. Gaby announced, "There will be another time for us to delve into your newly discovered abilities. For now, we advise you to take care of your family."

The room began turning dark, like a lamp dimming in the dead of night. Miles felt his legs turn wobbly before he slumped to the floor. He was conscious but disoriented.

We are not of your world. We are not of your world…

Miles heard the penthouse doors being flung open and realized the room smelled of smoke. He heard shrieking when the ceiling sprinklers blew water as a fire alarm echoed throughout the floor.

Water hit his face and body, but he didn't react. He remained supine, with his eyes half open, wondering at what he'd just experienced.

There was a male voice. "I told you, Miss Nina, lightning hit our building when we heard that loud boom."

A woman's face came into his view.

"Please don't be dead," she murmured repeatedly, until her mobile phone beeped and she picked it up.

Miles moved his arms after realizing he was among hotel staff.

"We found two guests in this room, Mr. Nichols," the woman reported. Then her eyes gleamed with relief. "They're breathing."

Miles vaguely saw her back on her mobile phone insisting, "There are two victims. Send an ambulance now!"

J . E L I Z A G A

17

The small community hospital was ill-equipped to receive emergencies that included possible electrocution and hysterical psychosis. Richelle was placed in the emergency room, while Miles, who remained conscious and alert, was sent to the information desk.

About to be interviewed by the triage nurse, he didn't quite know what information to provide. What should he share? A poltergeist attacked him and his wife, and they were saved by three strangers who said they were from another world, and who told him he had an ability to see and fight with spirits. Who would believe such a tale in a medical facility without committing him for mental evaluation?

Miles knew that the hotel staff arrived after the ambulance and listened as someone provided an "eyewitness" account. He heard that lightning struck near the resort and the occupants on the top floor were injured. That was going to be his answer.

"It was a beautiful day. We had gone up to check the top-floor suites," he started, when a scream reverberated through the quiet facility.

Richelle wanted to get out of her bed. Her arms flailed while she repeatedly demanded, "Get it off me. Get it off me!"

He ran to his wife's side. Two nurses held her, but she proved strong. "Rich, I'm here." He wrapped his arms around her. "I saw it. Listen to me. I saw it too."

Richelle lay back down, clutching her husband, her body racked by sobs. "Get it off me, Miles. Get it off me."

"It's gone, Rich," Miles soothed. But Richelle continued to be so terrified that she vomited. The attending physician and nurses took over to attend to her.

A medic arrived at the hospital, looking for a few supplies and heard the commotion. In less than a minute, the new doctor was speaking with Richelle's attending physician. They called Miles over to huddle.

"Mr. Penchant, my name is Dr. Dubois. I'm on a current assignment in this town. I came to get a few supplies and saw your wife in distress. I'd like to help her, if I can. Here is my ID," and he handed Miles his identification.

"I heard about a lightning strike and possible delusional visions from your wife. Is that correct?" He looked closely at Miles.

For some reason, Miles wanted to divulge every true thought he'd been keeping to the foreign doctor. But he chose words that he hoped would frame his reply as objectively as he could. "I'm not sure what happened myself. One moment, there was a lot of activity, and the next, the room turned dark and I nearly lost consciousness."

"That's a very interesting incident," the doctor started when Miles spoke.

"My wife—"

Dr. Dubois nodded. "I'd like to order tests for her before both of you are transported to the nearest city hospital. Also, the attending doctor gave me permission to peruse the pharmacy room for a sedative that I think her condition can use. Is that all right with you?"

Miles glanced at the attending physician, who nodded. The physician handed Richelle's chart to Dr. Dubois, who scribbled notes on it before handing it back. With a slight nod to both men, the medic walked wordlessly to the pharmacy room.

Miles returned to Richelle's side, holding close her still-trembling body. Dr. Dubois returned minutes later with a syringe and a calm and assuring manner, then explained and administered the medication to Richelle.

Miles sat in the chair across the bed where his wife lay resting. One of the nurses handed him a cup of coffee. He drank the warm liquid and felt his stomach relax. He inhaled deeply and slowly with relief, as though a thorn had been taken out of his chest.

After final instructions, Dr. Dubois said he needed to get back to his community service and left. The nurses took blood samples in order to complete the tests that could be performed there, while the rest would be done at the city hospital.

Momentarily at ease, he noticed his swollen knuckles and instantly recalled what happened at the resort. It was such a punch in the gut when he saw Richelle with another man, especially after their conversation in the car. But he knew that she wouldn't do that to him.

He remembered grabbing the fucker by the shoulders and throwing him to the floor. Everything seemed to slow down after that. The man had turned around, and it quickly dawned on Miles that the man looked like Miles. But that was nothing compared to the jolt he felt when the man morphed into something unholy and slithered across the floor.

And he'd fought it. He'd fought a monster!

He placed a hand over his dislocated shoulder and then the fractured rib. Both still throbbed and felt tender.

The three strangers—the woman said her name was Gaby. Did she really say they were from another world?

"Mr. Penchant?"

"Yes?" Miles looked up as the attending doctor sat beside him.

"We completed one of the tests that Dr. Dubois ordered. Your wife…" he started. "Your wife is pregnant."

18

The tears rolling down from the outer corners of Richelle's eyes tugged at Miles's heart after the attending physician relayed the news to them. Her condition would require special medical care, and there would be more monitoring ahead. But for now, she was calm and stable.

"I asked them to double-check, and they said the result was another positive," he informed her.

While the news of Richelle being pregnant rocked him, his wife's reaction was compounded by fear. "Why me? And what if it comes back?"

"I don't know yet, Rich, but I'll search for an answer," he promised. "We both saw it, and we were both attacked."

Richelle sobbed quietly. "I don't know what it did to me."

"It did nothing to you, honey. I got it off you, and" — Miles remembered what Gaby said and assured his wife — "it's not coming back, I promise."

She nodded before she changed the topic to the pregnancy. "I did have a couple of dizzy spells for the past month or two."

"And you didn't tell me?"

"I think they happened when I stood up too fast. I thought nothing of it. I was so focused on that business proposal."

He gently cleared strands of hair from her face, which were stuck on the wet lines of tears that had rolled down her cheeks. Rich squeezed his hand.

"This isn't like me, but I don't know what to feel right now," she admitted.

"You'll return to your old self, Rich." Miles pushed all thoughts in his mind aside. After the attending physician's revelation, he knew his life's purpose had changed.

"We'll be okay. I'll make sure you'll be safe and healthy." His eyes welled up as his heart begged him to release the fear and joy he felt at the same time. "Because we're going to have our baby."

19

*A*t the center of a rice field near the hospital where Miles and Richelle recuperated, three humanlike figures dressed in local clothing convened, hovering just above the sea of golden grains. From a distance, they looked like scarecrows standing at equal arm's lengths from each other.

The other two listened as Rafa provided new information. "His anomaly was traced back to your strand, Michael. And his clair senses are much stronger than any human's we've seen."

Michael remained silent, and his friend continued, "He didn't know he was an Anomaly. The only recorded incident mentioning him was with the old woman, who thought she discovered a young clairvoyant. However, he didn't recognize me in the emergency room."

"Probably was still in shock. He fought a supernatural entity with only his heart, without skill or knowledge," Gaby said. "That was impressive, but he needs to learn how to use his extraterrestrial abilities."

Michael wasn't enthusiastic about the discovery. "He will need more than guidance now that Lucifer knows what he is. The Anomaly will have to confront the creatures that will be sent to test him."

"Let him take care of his new family for a little bit," Rafa advised. "We can track and counter any activity directed at this human in the meantime."

Michael nodded. "I will resume contact at the appropriate time."

Gaby mused aloud, "Miles. In Latin, his name means soldier."

Michael turned his gaze toward her.

She continued, "I am increasingly curious about this discovery. We have not encountered such a strong iteration. What is the extent of his power? Would he survive crossing the portals? Can this human physically survive our realm? The possibility feels exciting."

Michael wanted to share in the excitement, but he had none for the moment. What he'd witnessed at the resort didn't impress him. Miles Penchant would be hounded by Lucifer's minions. He needed to be prepared to face that.

"He does not seem fit for the ability he possesses," Michael remarked. Yet when he muttered the Anomaly's name, he couldn't deny the spark of interest forming in his mind.

20

Five months later

*R*ichelle kept one hand under her belly while inspecting the crib Miles had ordered. It was custom-made of acacia wood, with beautiful carvings on the rails.

"Very nice, but can I rock it?" she commented.

"Of course, that's the first thing I made sure of," Miles replied, and proceeded to demonstrate.

She smiled, content as she scanned their bedroom, which now included baby furniture. She sighed at her husband's sweet gesture.

Her pregnancy led to an extended medical leave from the office. Miles was back at work but remained on desk duty. He didn't travel anymore. She was grateful that both companies gave them time to recover and prepare for the baby.

They'd had many discussions about what they'd experienced at the resort, and it always brought her fear. For the sake of the baby, they'd decided to put a hold on that and concentrate on becoming healthy. It seemed they'd switched personalities after what happened. She became introspective, while even-keeled Miles seemed more animated.

Her stomach moved.

"You like it, baby?" she asked her unborn, her voice tender with a little apprehension.

Her life nowadays went smoothly. She had the care of her spouse, their parents, and her doctors. She didn't have stress from work. But there'd been a couple of nightmares. Again, it was that long hallway and two doors. But this time, there was someone behind each door. She couldn't tell who they were. Her dream always ended before they were revealed.

She shared them with Miles, who was extra watchful around her. He said he'd seen nothing ever since that terrible night five months ago. She trusted his word.

She was thankful that life, so far, was back to normal.

21

Miles couldn't finish reviewing the wiring design assigned to him that day. He kept replaying what had happened at the resort in his mind. He left the office an hour early and stopped by a bar for a drink. He needed to calm down and be present for Richelle at home. Twice in the last few weeks, she'd mentioned a strange dream. And his gut didn't feel good every time she mentioned it.

He remembered what the mysterious being named Michael showed him about looking closely to see spirits. He'd been practicing. Still, he hadn't seen anything out of the ordinary around Rich.

He ordered a gin and tonic. Even after he took that first gulp, his mind returned to the three strange beings.

We are not of this world. We will meet another time. For now, we advise you to take care of your family.

Family—did they know Richelle was pregnant before I did?

He badly wanted answers, and wished he could meet those mysterious beings again, even though they were part of his violent paranormal experience.

He was still staring at his drink when the lights flickered. He straightened and looked up, thinking there'd been a blip in the electrical current.

The bar looked like a photograph. Everything hung in suspended animation. Heart racing, Miles blinked to make sure his eyes weren't deceiving him.

A voice nearby spoke. "Don't be alarmed. This is only in your mind."

A man sat a few seats away at the bar, which had been empty a second ago. "I too had been waiting for the opportune time to speak with you again. This seemed like the right moment."

He recognized the serious tone of the stranger's voice. "Michael."

The man replied, "I'm glad you remember."

Miles followed up quickly, "What did you do? I mean, how did you do this?" he asked as he looked around.

Michael remained in his seat as he said, "You are in stage one of falling asleep. I entered your thoughts at the point where your brain waves are between sleep and dreaming."

"If you're inside my head, then you know it's filled with questions."

Michael finally turned to face him. "To the brim, and I will answer them when we meet in person tonight."

"Tonight?" He went from feeling strangely excited to concerned. "Where? My wife is pregnant. I can't be away for too long."

"It won't take long. Five minutes of your time at most. A sign will show you the way." Michael got up and looked at Miles with a stare that punctured the areas of his mind where he hid his deepest thoughts. "I'll see you tonight."

Miles was still nodding when he heard a loud thud. He opened his eyes and saw the bartender had put down a glass of carbonated water in front of him with a smirk on his face. "You look like you dozed off. Dude who was just here said you could use some water."

Miles hurried home, but he didn't tell Richelle what had happened. He didn't want her to get upset about something related to their time at the resort.

J. ELIZAGA

22

Miles waited, but there was nothing out of the ordinary the entire evening. He went to bed wondering if he'd missed the sign already.

He woke up at 4:00 a.m. and headed to the bathroom, half awake, to empty his bladder. He was yawning while he waited to finish when he felt the familiar flutter in his stomach. He was drawn to look at the closed door, where a string of light ran around the perimeter, illuminating it.

His eyes widened at the sight, and he opened the bathroom door. The lights were off, and it was dark. It looked like his hallway, but it seemed longer and wider.

A figure appeared at the other end, and Michael's voice boomed around him. "Sorry I'm late. I had a council meeting to attend. See if you can walk over to this side, Miles."

It was the first time Miles felt his instinct move him to proceed instead of warning him to stay away. He took the first step. His foot landed a little unevenly on the ground. After that, he made a dash for it the rest of the way.

At the other end, he came upon an impeccably made thick glass door. He pushed it open and walked in. Michael, dressed casually in shades of gray, walked over to Miles. The two men shook hands. There was a table with two cups of coffee, but what caught Miles's attention were the lights outside, showcasing the rooftops of high-rise buildings. And he heard faint dance music.

He looked at Michael. "Are you in my head as what happened at the bar, or am I physically somewhere else?"

"Somewhere else. We're at the top-floor bar of a high-rise hotel in Hong Kong. Very nice, isn't it? They closed at three a.m."

"And how did I get here from my house?" Miles asked.

"I believe the scientific term humans use is a wormhole."

Miles's eyebrows rose as he picked up the wonderful scent of coffee.

"Help yourself to coffee," Michael offered as he gestured him to sit down. "I see you know about wormholes."

"Only in passing." Miles shook his head to make room for the information he'd just received.

"Drink your coffee while I talk," Michael said.

Miles sat down and took a sip. "I don't like leaving my wife for long periods of time."

"I'll do my best to keep it short," Michael responded before finishing his coffee in one swig.

"Gaby, Rafa, and I, are citizens of the planet Kalumegn, located outside your universe," Michael shared.

"You look human. Yet, you say you're from another universe. It's confusing my brain. I guess I was expecting a, well, different look, or being," Miles admitted.

"If this will help," Michael replied. His dark-skinned human form disintegrated until what remained was a translucent being encased in a gel-like covering. But his eyes stood out most. The sclera was black instead of the white that humans had. And what must be the iris was also black with a visibly silvery outline that changed colors.

Miles stood up, aghast.

"You should sit down again, Miles. You look like you'll pass out. This takes some getting used to."

Miles sat down, but remained staring at the alien being in front of him. "I guess I asked for it. How did... Where are you... No, that's Kalumegn, you said that already. Is Michael really your name?" was all he could think of.

"It's the closest sound to my name," Michael replied calmly.

Miles wasn't sure how he felt, but forced himself to settle down and speak with more coherence. "How did you find me at the resort? What were you doing, I guess, here on Earth?"

"We were tracking the entity you fought, not you. Normally, we don't interact with humans. But when you grabbed Rafa's arm and didn't disintegrate, we determined you were an Anomaly." Michael sat across from Miles before he continued. "You are human, but there was an aberration in your genome that caused the special abilities you possess. Do you remember what you can do?"

Miles nodded. "I can touch spirits as though they were solid."

"More accurately, you can interact with beings of energy from a different dimension. And a few moments ago, you went through a wormhole, also unharmed," Michael said. "You are indeed an Anomaly; one we have not encountered before."

Though the coffee helped, Miles was barely keeping up with what Michael had just said. "My genome, aliens, and wormholes," he whispered to himself before asking aloud, "I thought I fought a poltergeist at the resort. How does that relate to aliens and wormholes? And how did you make a wormhole from my house in Manila to a high-rise in Hong Kong?"

"I'll answer the second question first. I didn't create the wormhole. You did."

Miles's eyebrows went up again.

"What do you remember about the sign you were waiting for?" Michael asked.

"I waited for something to happen all evening, until my wife and I went to sleep. Then I got up at around four to go to the bathroom. I felt obliged to look at the door, and a thin line of light illuminated its perimeter."

"When your mind was ready, you saw the door. Where do you want to go after this meeting?" Michael asked.

"Home," Miles replied.

"Focus on that, then blink once," Michael instructed.

As soon as Miles blinked, his vision changed, and it alarmed him so much that he stood up again. He rubbed his eyes and swiped his hands in front of him, but his vision remained the same. "What are these grid lines in front of everything? How do I turn this off? Wait, I've seen these before." His tone rose with fear.

"No need to be alarmed. That is the fabric of time and space. It's everywhere, as you can see. And if you want to travel through a wormhole, let your mind show you the portal to where you want to go. Don't pick any random point in time and space, and be careful you don't fracture the continuity."

It was disorienting, but he took a deep breath to steady himself. Then he looked straight ahead and moved his head to minimize the vertigo he started to get. But when his gaze came upon the thick glass door, its perimeter glowed with the same thin line of light. "I see it."

"Good," Michael affirmed. "Once you have identified the portal, your sight will return to normal with another blink."

Miles blinked again, sighing as his vision returned to normal.

But just as he looked at Michael with a relieved smile, he saw a shadow move behind him. A second later, Michael had his hand firmly on a creature. Once again, Miles heard the unearthly wail. His heart nearly dropped out of his chest. He watched as Michael smashed the creature hard on the wall until the wailing turned into a language he understood.

"Please, I am free from his control," the shadow implored. Michael released his grip, and the shadow floated away. Miles sat back down, his knees weak and his body trembling.

"They can come back," he whispered, almost to himself. He'd promised Richelle those entities wouldn't return.

"I'll answer the first question now. It goes back to your abilities as an Anomaly. You can see beings of energy, including beings who are no longer living. This is why you were able to play with Mrs. Rosa's dogs when you were a young boy," Michael explained.

Miles wasn't really paying attention. "I promised my wife those monsters wouldn't come back. Are they following us? Richelle is due to give birth in less than three months."

"You will be tested, Miles," Michael answered.

Miles buried his face in his hands. He had to protect Richelle from this craziness. But there was something in what Michael said. "Wait, if I can see beings of energy, and I can see you and I didn't die when I grabbed Rafa's arm, are you also beings of energy?"

"We're close to it, but no. If we were, we would be one with the universe," Michael replied.

"I can't have those monsters terrifying my wife again," Miles started.

"My advice would be to prepare yourself." Michael seemed to have read his mind.

"What do I need to do?"

Michael took a moment. "It won't be easy, Anomaly. We will prepare gradually as your body adjusts. For the rest of this week, practice invoking the grid lines on and off and jumping to different locations. You need to be able to do that efficiently and in the blink of an eye. We will meet again next week."

Miles nodded. "I'm not sure what I'm agreeing to, but I trust you." He stood. With home in mind, he turned away from Michael and anxiously blinked. The grid lines appeared. After he saw the illuminated door, he blinked again to clear them from his vision.

With a final nod to Michael, Miles left and walked into the hallway. He opened the bathroom door and was back in their bedroom. He read the luminous digits on their alarm clock. 4:10 a.m.

It was as Michael said, about five minutes had passed.

I'm an Anomaly?

After he slid gently back into bed and looked at his wife, whose shoulders moved up and down with each breath, his mood changed abruptly to worry. Richelle and the baby must remain safe at all costs.

J. ELIZAGA

23

Whether he was at the office or at home, Miles practiced conjuring the grid lines every time he went to the bathroom. But on the fourth day, he decided to go through the portal and visit a certain location...the resort in the Palawan Island where he and Richelle had their honeymoon.

He wanted to arrive in the evening, when his appearance would be camouflaged by the darkness. He visualized the time and place until he saw the grid lines and the illuminated portal.

After taking a deep breath, he stepped through. He was unsteady on his feet, but the faster he walked, the steadier he felt. He appeared out of the portal in the island at night, right under the resort's unlit archway.

He walked around the property grounds lit by tiki torches as though he were a guest. He lingered at the shoreline, where he sat on fine-grain white sands, listened to the waves rushing in and moving away and looked at the cloudless star-filled sky.

Ready to travel back, he nervously invoked the grid lines to return to the office. They appeared, but it took several seconds for the portal to illuminate.

He was back in the men's washroom in time to place his hands under the running water as a coworker walked in.

For a short while, he felt buoyed by his new routine.

After the Palawan Island visit, he traveled back and forth even more. He returned to the top-floor bar in Hong Kong. He walked the grounds at Angkor Wat in Cambodia, joined a tour group in New York City, and visited the Sagrada Familia in Barcelona.

Over the first week, he practiced at least twice a day, improving his speed in switching the grid lines on and off and finding the portals.

He wanted to be ready for his next meeting with Michael.

On Monday morning of the following week, after he returned home from the office, his instincts were pushing him to go to the bedroom while Richelle was in the kitchen. As soon as he dropped a kiss on her cheek, he started unbuttoning his shirt on the way to change clothes. But as he approached their bedroom, the grid lines appeared before their door, illuminated. He closed his eyes, buttoned up his shirt, and opened the door.

It was eerie to find the bedroom dark and stretched diagonally, where Michael stood at the farthest corner of the room.

"I thought we might go together to the next destination," Michael offered.

"Taking me to a different dimension," Miles started. "Like Virgil with Dante?" He caught the uplift of Michael's eyebrows. "Some engineers like a little bit of literature… no, actually, it was a video game. "

"Except Dante wasn't an Anomaly. He needed assistance to cross into the other dimension. The river Acheron was actually a wormhole. He had to use a transport pod to cross it. And Virgil was one of our citizens," Michael shared.

The two continued walking into the darkness. Miles noted a change in the lighting as they made their way through the wormhole.

"I haven't read about that backstory. What more can you share?" But when they reached the end of the portal, Miles forgot what he had asked. They stood on the grounds of a massive, abandoned building in the middle of the night.

"Where are we?" he whispered. The air was chilly, and the silence and the stillness felt taut.

"We are in front of one of the most haunted places in Czechoslovakia," Michael answered. "I assume you understand why I brought you here."

Miles nodded, "Are we talking about the lingering energies of deceased humans that remain on Earth—in other words, ghosts?"

Michael nodded. "You're getting used to switching the grid lines on and off. Perhaps if you get used to these entities, your fear wouldn't hold you back, even though you hold on to it."

Miles straightened. "We were having a moment a second ago. Now it just became serious. So what do I do?"

"Before doing comes understanding," Michael began. "I'll explain as we reach the door."

The two men walked toward the entrance.

"In this abandoned area, spirits were left in limbo because something tied them to this place. It's usually an extreme experience. But the ones who attack are controlled by a greater force."

Miles opened his mouth to ask what "greater force" meant when a luminous orb darted from a tree to a window on the ground floor. Michael seemed to have ignored it. Miles kept his cool and forced himself to pay attention. As they came closer to the building, he could hear wailing voices coming from the inside.

"By the law of physics, these spirits are not destroyed, but to remove the control over them, you will need to use some force." Michael had barely finished when a luminous orb came out of nowhere and hit them. He caught it with his hand and smashed it violently against the wall. More wailing echoed.

But then Miles heard a soft voice. "Please."

Michael stopped and released his grip on the orb. It floated away.

Miles felt the sweat on his upper lip in the dead of the chilly night as Michael gave him pointers. "Remember that these orbs, shadows, or mutations of various forms do not feel physical pain. What you must do is break them from what's possessing them."

"By smashing them."

"With significant force, yes," Michael confirmed. "However, you will need to learn to control your emotions. They will test you, and hurt you, until you want to destroy them with your hands. But you must let them go once they are no longer possessed."

"Possessed and controlled. Who or what is controlling them?"

Michael looked away, seeming deep in thought for a second before his stoic expression returned. "My nemesis."

They stopped in front of a pair of heavy intricately carved wooden doors. Miles's heartbeat pounded in his ears. Michael raised his hand in front of the doors before turning to him. "Whatever you encounter, remember that I am with you."

Miles wanted to freak out. Michael's words sounded like jargon—spirits and laws of physics, smash them to release the force controlling them.

But a sense of warmth radiated from his gut to his shoulders. It calmed him. A second ago, he wanted to turn back and run away as fast as he could. Now, his feet were steady on the creaking wood floors.

The door opened, and cold musty air hit his face. A resonating wail echoed, while what was left of a giant chandelier moved slightly.

The two men entered. Miles thought his vision adjusted to the darkness when he saw the chandelier moving. Or it could be light from the moon outside coming through the windows—

He was struck hard on his shoulder and fell to his knees. Michael's voice rang through the darkness. "Get up."

Miles scrambled up when he heard Michael's voice again. "Coming in left."

He faced left, swung his arm hard, and hit nothing like a drunk asking for a fight. Michael commanded, "Focus."

Three different voices spoke his name amid the hissing and wailing. "Miles...Penchant..."

Memories of terror at the resort and what was happening to him at the moment crammed his mind. Disoriented, he sensed something would come from the right. Then he saw it from his periphery: a grayish figure on its hands and feet coming at him like a small animal moving with surprising speed. But when the figure straightened up, it was taller than him.

The creature jumped from about fifteen feet away. Miles placed one foot behind him, placing distance between his legs for stability.

He swung an arm and hit the creature. It grunted. But quickly, it had Miles by the neck, attempting to raise him off the floor.

"Use your hands, not your fist," came the voice in the darkness.

Miles struggled to breathe, but he managed to get one hand around the creature's torso area.

"Squeeze without mercy."

Miles felt the creature's grasp loosen, just a little. It was enough. He raised his other hand and seized the creature by its head. It wailed loudly as he increased the pressure, but its body continued writhing until it connected to Miles's stomach with a kick and broke free.

As Miles fell backward, he saw Michael grab the shadow figure. In one blink, Michael moved from where he stood with the creature to the heavy doors. He smashed the shadow figure against the door so hard that the wood creaked.

A limp shadow floated away from Michael's hands.

Miles stood, despite shaking knees. Michael returned to his side.

"Your courage is evident," Michael said. "But you lack skill and practice."

Miles didn't feel good after what happened. For the second time in his life, he wasn't able to stop a paranormal monster.

24

Miles didn't travel through a wormhole over the next few days. At different times since his last meeting with Michael, an illuminated door appeared, beckoning him to cross to the other side, but he held back.

One of Richelle's coworkers contacted him. They were planning a surprise baby shower for her at a restaurant. Miles was tasked with keeping the surprise from his wife while knowing all the details. That kept him grounded and gratefully occupied with something other than what weighed heavily on his mind.

During dinner, he watched Richelle eat and coo at her belly. Maybe it was the angle of the overhead lamp, but he thought she looked radiant and glowing. They had two and a half more months to go.

He wasn't sure how to handle having a family and learning to be this extraterrestrial anomaly. He kicked himself for putting aside the parenting books he'd been reading in favor of maps and time with Michael.

They will test you, and hurt you…

Yet, he was equally worried about what the unknown entities could do to his family.

"Dammit," he muttered. There didn't seem to be a pick-one option. It had to be both. Alone in the kitchen, Miles closed his eyes and thought of his encounter at the haunted castle. He opened his eyes and surveyed the grid lines until one intersection caught his eye. The tiny point where two lines met illuminated and then another point lit, and another until a rectangle formed, drawing a portal.

With a deep breath, he proceeded to go through the other side, unsure where he would be taken, but hopeful that Michael was there.

Moments later, he was standing at the opening of a cave, which was large enough to fit a trailer truck. A cool breeze blew across his body from behind. He turned around and surveyed the rest of the area, careful not to step over the edge of the cave. He was in an arid climate but didn't know where. Below where he stood, a set of buildings carved in the face of a sheer rock cliff with colorfully painted domes attracted his attention.

"Miles, glad you could make it." Michael spoke behind him.

He turned around, inwardly relieved. "I think it was inevitable. But I assume you already knew."

Michael shook his head. "You always have a choice. But I hoped you'd come back."

It was a strange feeling of brotherhood with someone who wasn't human. "Where are we? This is breathtaking."

"An old monastery in the Judean desert. This cave is a special place," Michael replied.

"What makes it special?"

"There is a protective element here. Our tracking system is not able to penetrate this location, which makes it a good hiding place while you train."

They walked deeper into the cave, and down a narrow flight of stairs. There was basic lighting as they reached an inner chamber.

Michael stopped at the entryway. Inside, an old man wearing a faded brown robe sat with his eyes closed. But he stood, and a smile broke on his face before he opened his eyes. Miles realized he could be meeting a monk.

"Old friend," the man greeted.

Michael took the diminutive man's shoulders and gave him a brief hug. "Master, thank you for meeting with us, away from your home in the East."

Miles realized he hadn't actually seen the man walk toward them.

"This is Miles," Michael introduced. Miles extended his hand. The man's eyebrows went up, and Miles saw his eyes were mostly white, as someone afflicted with cataracts.

"Human," he whispered.

"A newly discovered Anomaly, and we need your help," Michael stated. Miles listened intently as their conversation continued.

"What kind of help do you seek?" the monk asked as he moved his head to follow who was talking.

"To prepare him to deal with the controlled entities," Michael said.

"I have a wife and child on the way," Miles interrupted.

"When are you expecting your child?" the monk asked.

"In about ten weeks," Miles replied.

The monk mused quietly for a second before stating, "Training shall be condensed, but not impossible."

Miles smirked. "You haven't seen me yet. I'm sorry I didn't catch your name, sir."

"I am Darma. You may call me Mister D, or the Big D. However, I don't like being called Dude," he answered. When Miles gave no reply and continued staring at him, Darma looked at Michael and said, "He takes after you. Quite a serious young man."

It was the first time Miles saw Michael's face relax. But Darma had already turned his attention back to him. "You must learn to live in the lightness as well as the darkness. I expect to see you here at this time for the next thirty days."

Am I ready for this?

It was as though he read Miles's thoughts. "There is no turning back. This is the burden of being an Anomaly, young man." A wooden stick about five feet long appeared in his hands out of nowhere and drew a rectangle in the air. "Tomorrow, you must wear clothes suitable for physical activity and nourish yourself with food and water."

Miles returned to their kitchen, thirsty from the heat of the desert. He could hear Richelle humming loudly from their bedroom. More than being anxious about the old man's training, he wanted to spill everything that happened to him to her.

Yet after he cleared his throat, he knew he couldn't tell her. Instead, he asked aloud what vegetables he could start chopping. What good would knowing bring her? She'd been doing well after her terrifying experience. And they were so close to having their dream family.

25

Miles wondered how much extra sweat the pain from walking on raw blistered feet for hours brought. After six hours, the landscape looked the same, dry stony sand everywhere. But he continued along the path until he was the only person left walking.

He walked with tourists, as men with donkeys offered everyone on the road a moment to rest their legs and feet while they sat on the animals that carried them up the trail. The tourists took the offer, but he didn't.

It was sunset, and the orange sky was darkening far out on the horizon. The path on the side of the mountains turned shadowy. He was tempted to use a wormhole from where he stood to go back to the cave. He closed his eyes and for a second fought the urge to conjure the grid lines.

The sun was long set when he reached the cave. Darma gave him a nod for completing his task, then told him to return the following day for a new task.

"There's no way I'll be able to do the next session in this condition," he said to himself as he looked for a pain reliever in their medicine cabinet at home.

Over the next seven days, Miles wished he'd kept up his basketball skills from many years ago. His body was subjected to exercises from stretching to crescent kicks and fingertip push-ups, which he found most difficult. He lifted large rocks and smashed them against the mountainside as hard as he could. The monk also taught him meditation, to increase his attentiveness to the messages from his instincts and to practice sensing Richelle from his mind.

"Remember, you have to be able to destroy whatever control has been placed on these entities. Set them free," Darma explained. "That requires upper body strength, agile footwork and extraordinary speed and focus. Next week, we will proceed to fighting techniques."

He was famished every time he returned from training. He ate more than usual, and told Richelle that he too was eating for the baby. But at the end of the week, he'd lost five pounds.

By the second week, Miles settled on a schedule to train up to six hours daily with the old man, who taught him eighteen stances to use against different entities. Over half of the moves were excruciating to perform.

"Unfortunately, you do not have the luxury of years of training," Darma stated. "And your only weapons are your hands and feet."

By far, the most important move he learned was to crouch down very low so that he sat on one of his calves while the other leg was crossed over the opposite knee. It allowed him to get up very quickly while he took a moment to rest or seek his instinct. After assuming the position, Darma instructed him to close his eyes and open his mind.

"You must catch your instinct's guidance faster, young man. You don't have a millisecond to lose when entities are on the attack," Darma said.

The training days were difficult: stretch, push, lift, do the eighteen stances, and meditate. But Miles oddly savored every moment.

Richelle had been doing well. They were going to Lamaze classes. Her surprise baby shower was a success. Having her friends around gave her more courage to face childbirth. There was nothing pressing on his mind, and it opened during his meditations. His body responded more quickly to his instinct. In the past, it would take him a few minutes of looking around to figure out why he was drawn to something, but now, he could hear his instinct's guidance clearly and more quickly, as though a voice was describing what would happen next in his ear.

Miles started week four on time in the cave. But the master wasn't there. Miles waited and, after a minute, decided to start without him. He warmed up, then followed with practicing the eighteen stances. As he did the rest-and-crouch stance, he felt a presence dart to his side. His hands automatically formed into stiff open palms.

As soon as Miles heard the wail, he stood and remained still until with practiced speed, he extended one of his arms and grabbed a large gray figure zigzagging toward him. Different sounds echoed in the cave. Soon, he recognized a head and then a body: an entity with no face. Miles held on, and as the head mutated into a monstrous form, he squeezed as hard as he could. The entity disappeared in his hands. Miles looked around, alert for another attack. But it was Darma who appeared at the entrance of the cave. His robe was disheveled, but there was a smile on his face. "I liked the speed of your reflexes and the strength of your hands, Anomaly. And you look less flabby."

It was true, Miles had to admit. His muscles had hardened from the training. They weren't as bulky as a weight lifter, but sinewy.

"It's due to your training." Miles bowed his head in gratitude.

"You are missing one more thing, young man," the monk started. At once, Miles was all eyes and ears. "You need fire in your heart. It has to be automatic when you encounter danger."

Miles nodded. He understood what his teacher meant, but he hadn't had a chance to fight an entity since he started training four weeks ago. The last encounter he'd had was at the haunted castle when an entity kicked him and broke free from his grip.

"Miles." A female voice called as though she was on loudspeaker, but far away. His heart skipped, and the hair on the back of his neck stood up.

"Richelle," he answered aloud.

"Very strong clairaudience," Darma exclaimed. "Is she—"

"My wife." Miles disappeared from the cave in less than a second.

J. ELIZAGA

26

*R*ichelle squinted from the glare of a singular light above. She hadn't seen the sun so bright and so close before. It was a beautiful day to run the marathon. She could see runners alongside her in their green outfits. And she was ready to run with them; she'd prepared for months for this. She could see the sign of the finish line just above the hill.

It felt odd that she thought she was pregnant, and her water broke in the bathroom. She looked down at her belly. It didn't look pregnant. She continued jogging at a comfortable pace.

She caught the whiff of sweet amber, and a sense of familiarity returned. Could it be? It had been nearly a year since—

"Richelle Penchant, you didn't tell me you ran marathons," Luc spoke from her side. She glanced at her left shoulder and found him jogging near her. She remembered she always found him well-dressed. This time, it was refreshing to see him in running attire with an unshaven face.

"Luc, what a strange coincidence you're here too," she greeted back.

"Self-employment has afforded me more personal time. I'm Luc, consultant for hire," he replied with a slight theatrical bow. Richelle gave him a thumbs-up but didn't reply. She continued jogging with her eyes on the finish line.

"What placement are you going for? You're doing well on your speed," Luc remarked.

Richelle smiled. "Oh, not vying for anything. This is for my personal goal only, to reach the finish line."

"If you're not watching your time, can we stop for a second? My legs are cramping up," he proposed as he slowed to a fast walk.

Richelle turned around and hovered near him but kept jogging in place. A runner passing by turned around and called out, "Hey, don't stop now, or your muscles will turn cold. Keep going. We're nearly there."

Richelle turned to look at the runner. The woman had one of the most beautiful faces she'd ever seen. It was breathtaking. But her voice sounded oddly familiar. "Have I met you before?"

"Maybe, I'm not sure," the woman answered diplomatically. "Don't hang out with a slacker, or you'll fall back and quit the race."

Luc hissed at the woman. "Fine, just give me a second to take a drink." He produced a bottle of ice-cold water, and Richelle looked longingly at it. A second later, she grabbed her stomach as though she were in pain.

"Are you okay?" The woman stood by Richelle's right shoulder. "Look, there's plenty of ice water, juice, and vitamin drinks at the finish line. What's your name, by the way? I'm Gaby."

"Richelle. I'm okay. I felt an odd sensation in my stomach. Yeah, we better keep running. His water just looked tempting for a second," she admitted.

"That's because you're tired, Rich," Luc exclaimed before he twisted the cap off his bottle and offered it to her. "Here, take a sip. It's going to refresh you. Taking a breather isn't going to kill you."

But Gaby spoke quickly. "Listen, it's less than a mile up the hill. I'll pace with you, but you have to keep going and focus on the finish line."

Richelle looked back and forth between Luc and Gaby. The two looked good together. Maybe she could be a matchmaker after this race. But the sensation in her stomach returned with another wave. She bent over, dizzy and nauseous.

"Oh, for crying out loud." Luc held her arm. "Drink some water now, child."

Gaby was equally insistent. "I'll carry you to the finish, Richelle. You can do it."

But the hot glare from the sun was beating down on her forehead. Richelle took the bottle from Luc's hand and raised it to her lips. She poured water into her mouth.

Luc stepped back with a triumphant grin on his face. "What did I tell you before? I can give you what you want, always."

As soon as she heard those words, Richelle violently spit out the water and ran away. She heard Luc shouting in anger, but Gaby was beside her, with an arm around her shoulders. Richelle heard voices from the sky: "Pressure's dropping. How's the baby doing? Cleaning her up now."

Baby?

Richelle was pulled violently back. She fell. When she looked, there were elongated spiny arms holding her feet. Then she watched as Luc mutated into a familiar slithering monster from her past. She didn't remember screaming.

"You committed to drink. You committed to me. Your soul is mine!" the monster growled.

Suddenly, Gaby landed with a heavy thud in front of them and punched the monster. It momentarily loosened its hold, and Richelle broke free. She ran toward Gaby, but another long spiny extremity coiled around her legs and dragged her back. The gravel scraped the skin on her legs raw.

Richelle clutched her chest as Gaby jumped and landed in front of the creature again.

And then the voices in the sky became louder. "It's a crash, clear everyone, clear."

Gaby held her arm out, and the monster froze in suspended animation. "Enough," she commanded.

Richelle's chest felt so heavy that she couldn't get up. She felt weak, but something in her mind cleared as she looked at Gaby's face. "I remember your voice," she whispered. "I've had enough of these strange dreams, so I'll do something unusual this time."

It was difficult to concentrate with beeping sounds everywhere, but she reached into her chest and pulled out a small red orb. She handed it to Gaby, who seemed taken aback before taking the orb from her.

"That's a substantial chunk of your life force."

Richelle answered breathlessly, "It's half of my heart. Please give this to my husband. His name is Miles Penchant."

The slithering poltergeist behind them wailed, "You took the part I want. I'm no longer interested."

Gaby nodded and held on to the orb. Richelle sighed and let her body relax, keeping her eyes closed as she floated toward the finish line.

J. ELIZAGA

27

Nurses quickly escorted Miles out of the operating room when Richelle's heart started crashing during her caesarian procedure. He demanded to know what was happening, but the only answer he received was, "Sir, you need to leave now."

The wait was agonizing. Hours later, the lead surgeon broke the news. "Your wife went into cardiac arrest. We got her heart beating again, but her vitals right now are weak. Her blood pressure keeps fluctuating. We are monitoring it very closely. We're running tests. She's unconscious at the moment."

The doctor's words hadn't fully registered in his mind, even though he could hear his mother-in-law weeping loudly behind him.

Miles was taken to a private room to be with his daughter, and only when he felt the baby in his arms did the doctor's words sink in.

His legs had no strength. He was glad to be sitting down. He took a deep breath as his daughter lay quietly.

They hadn't even settled on a name. They wanted to get to know her personality first.

The tears flowed without him noticing. He sat staring at his child with the most wonder a parent could, and yet his heart was broken for Richelle.

He heard the soft thud of the door to the private room closing. He knew the nurse had given him a few minutes to be with their new baby. Oh, she was so very beautiful and delicate.

"Your mom and I waited seven years to finally have you," Miles whispered. "So tell her to wake up and join our party." He sniffled.

He comforted himself and his newborn in the silence of the room, cradling her, rocking his body gently.

As he settled in the chair and leaned his shoulders back, he looked up and saw the door of the room illuminated. Gaby walked in and looked at him, but in less than a blink of an eye, she was gone again.

Miles wasn't sure if he had indeed seen her, or if his mind was desperate.

Then he heard, "Miles, I gave it to Gaby."

Richelle's voice was faint but distinct. Maybe she'd woken up and was calling him. But how did she know Gaby's name?

A portal must be open, and Rich is somehow on the other side with Gaby.

The nurse knocked softly on the door. Miles returned their baby to her and said, "Do you mind if I use the bathroom here? I'll be right out."

She nodded without looking at him. Miles thanked her.

As soon as the door closed, the bathroom door illuminated. He opened it and walked through.

Gaby moved quickly toward the end of the portal in her natural form with the luminous sheen on her skin covered by a dark gray uniform. He called her name, and she turned around. Dots of light pulsed on her forehead, but Miles was most drawn to her eyes. The irises were very large, and they changed colors in quick succession.

"You look formidable," Miles couldn't stop himself from saying.

"And you're not freaking out at my appearance, human. Listen, I have to reach Clos Friga, but Richelle wanted this for you." She produced a small glowing red orb and held it out to Miles. "This is half of her heart."

Miles recited Richelle's usual retort. "The half which likes to fight. Richelle, why did you—"

"Take it and give it back to her, and you two may have the life you long dreamed of," she interrupted.

Miles nodded and took the orb. He was about to turn around when the other end of the wormhole flared up in bright orange. Little dark figures appeared in front of the blazing light. And they appeared to be moving.

"Go now." Gaby pushed, but Miles remained transfixed by a battalion coming closer to them. He recognized they were entities, and they didn't look like a welcoming committee.

"Let me stay until you reach the other side," he said. He opened his jacket and slid the orb inside to free both hands.

But the glowing orb instead went through his chest. In a second, he bent over with pain. Then he started to feel indignant at having to fight when all he wanted was to return to his wife and newborn.

Who the fuck do these ugly pieces of shit think they are? I'm not going to be a victim here. If they want a fight, I'll give them one.

He ran after Gaby, who was already on the offensive. He could see the entities clearly now. Every manifestation of slithering, tentacled, and fanged aberration raced toward them, but Gaby's strides didn't miss a beat.

He didn't blink in case he missed anything. That was when she jerked her arm forward, and a wave of energy passed through his body. The ground underneath him shook. The force threw him to the ground, along with about three-quarters of the monsters. After they violently hit the ground, they turned into gray mists, and floated away, but the remaining ones got up and surged toward them.

"Miles, don't breathe here. This isn't Earth. Your human breath will drive the trapped souls into a frenzy," Gaby shouted over her shoulder.

"Trapped souls? Human breath—what—why?" Miles asked without looking at her. His senses were alert and focused on a group of shadow creatures marching closer to them.

"They will smell hope," Gaby answered.

Miles pursed his lips shut, even though he didn't get how his breath could smell of hope.

A shadow moved to his right and jumped toward him, but Miles already turned and smacked it with his fist. Then he quickly grabbed and smashed it to the ground with no second thought. He heard it sigh and let it go, only to see two more entities in front of him.

He ducked away from a tentacle, elbowed a half beast, and kicked another tentacle. He grabbed the head of the half beast with one hand, and the head of the slithering, tentacled entity with his other hand and smashed them against each other. A loud wail and a growl came out, followed by sighs.

He and Gaby continued fighting as they moved closer to the end of the wormhole, until there was nothing left attacking them.

Gaby moved ahead of him when Miles stepped back. "I think we released everyone, Gaby. I'm going back—"

His feet came off the ground, and his body torpedoed until it landed hard.

By a miracle, Miles kept his mouth shut even though the wind was nearly knocked out of him. He straightened up to the sound of fighting and wailing. There were orbs and gray mists everywhere of all sizes, colliding with one another and throwing sparks in unending chaos.

His skin prickled as if a thousand heated needles rushed through his body. He winced and dropped to his knees, but the sensation was short-lived. He staggered until he stood again with Gaby's help.

"You are indeed an Anomaly." She pulled him upright.

What in hell is this?

"Exactly," Gaby looked at him. "I can hear your thoughts. Keep speaking with your mind."

Exactly what? Where are we?

She nodded. "This is the planet Clos Friga, which you call 'hell.'"

28

G aby quickly ripped a cord from her waist and clamped it to his. "However, you have no avionic abilities. You will need a little help."

What are those dots of light on your forehead about?

"There is an attempted escape going on here. I'm receiving updates as we speak," she answered when a group of shadow creatures came from behind them. Gaby neutralized them with one swish of her arm, but Miles heard gnarly voices becoming louder.

Gaby glanced in the direction of the voices. "We should run to the crevice and descend. You have a better chance at finding a spot to hide down there. Stay put until one of us comes back for you."

Descend the crevice?

"Welcome to your baptism by fire." Gaby announced. "Shall we?"

They ran across a barren field, both evading entities that crossed their paths until Gaby grabbed his arm to stop. Miles stood at the edge of the largest opening in the ground he'd ever seen.

"Press your toes forward to move down, keep them straight to hover, lean forward to move straight, and press your heel down to ascend," she explained. "The more you press, the faster you go."

Like a Segway, I think.

"Yes, Anomaly. Let's go," Gaby urged.

But he didn't move immediately. He was thinking of his newborn child.

Gaby looked at him. When she spoke, her voice sounded calm but confident. "A human once said if you were going through hell, keep going. We'll get you back to your family, but we can't get out of here until the situation is resolved."

Miles nodded.

Gaby walked beyond the edge, turned around, and signaled him to follow. Nervously, he peered over the edge. It looked dizzying, but his gaze gravitated toward a ball of blue-white light at the bottom that shone obtrusively bright.

What's that?

"That's Michael's nemesis," she answered. "And it is attempting to escape."

Why are we going there again?

"To hide you in a cave. No one knows you are here unless you breathe," Gaby replied quickly.

The response surprised him so much that he took a step forward to get a better look without realizing he'd gone beyond the rim as well.

"Two more steps, and then press the toe down, easy," he heard her say.

Miles gingerly pressed his toes down and moved a few feet lower. Gaby had already moved farther than he did. He adjusted his feet, and, after getting used to the movement, he caught up with her.

They descended quickly, with Gaby occasionally fending off an entity on a collision course with them. They'd gone far down without stopping when Miles realized there were separate levels of caverns. He looked up, trying to count how many levels they'd passed.

"Here, Anomaly," Gaby said. Miles pressed his heels a little too quickly, and she grabbed his arm again.

They hovered in front of a dark opening. Gaby went in, and Miles followed. It was just tall enough for Miles to stand up, but Gaby morphed into the woman he'd met at the resort. In human form, she could fit in the cave.

"This space will be sufficient until we have the situation under control. Stay here," she directed.

He nodded and looked outside, where the bluish-white light illuminated the area.

What's reflecting so much light?

"The bottom is a layer of ancient ice—" A powerful earthquake shook the cave, throwing Miles to the ground. In an instant, Gaby disappeared from sight.

A great wailing reverberated from outside. Something metallic flew past the opening. Rather than stick his nose out and seek the action, he decided to stay put and on alert.

He sat in the crouching stance Master Darma taught him, but kept his eyes open. He theorized he hadn't gasped for air because on Earth, it had only been a minute or two—

His instinct sounded the alarm. A gray mist entered the cave. Miles got to his feet. The mist turned into a slithering entity that looked similar to the one in his memory. And his memory gave rise to anger. He clenched his fists.

I'll fight this one with all my heart, Rich.

The monster lunged to grab his leg, but he answered it with a kick to its limb that was attempting to grab him. The monster wailed ferociously. There was no circling and waiting for the next strike. He ran, then jumped on the wall, did a somersault, and pounced on the monster. His fingers clamped on the side of its head. As soon as he landed, he smashed the monster into the ground. He smashed it again. And again.

"Please," a voice whimpered.

His arm stopped moving, but his entire body shook with the desire to beat it to a pulp.

Without realizing, he'd walked to the entrance of the cave without releasing the gray figure from his grasp. He stood and peered out when something large hit the mountain near where he stood. The force shook the ground beneath his feet. Miles let go of the limp entity.

He swiveled at the edge of the cave's entrance and fell out.

29

A record-setting free-fall skydive from the stratosphere televised in 2012 flashed in his mind. Unlike a skydiver, Miles couldn't remain upright. He continued to spiral down until he landed hip first, on his back with a loud thud.

Surprisingly, his mouth remained shut. He didn't move, but his eyes remained open, staring at the hectic activity far above him, like watching an alien invasion.

A giant metallic half body fought with another giant, which he recognized as Michael.

Michael's nemesis is a machine?

The creature had transformed its arms into different handheld weapons. One was a sword and the other a flail. Meanwhile, Michael held a metallic rod that buzzed with sparks every time it made contact with the creature's body.

Gaby and the other beings of Kalumegn fought with the entities trying to get to Michael. She was mighty. One forceful swing of her arm caused a visible wave of energy that smashed a line of them against the rock face. Still, the orbs and entities kept pushing their attack.

From his vantage point, Miles realized the situation wouldn't calm down soon, but he needed to return home. It was time to get up and do something. He turned around and faced down so he could push himself up.

He accidentally exhaled as he moved.

Steam rose from the icy floor where he breathed. An animal growled in the distance. Miles's heart sank as he realized what he'd done. Fiery red eyes flashed against the darkness, and then he heard the sound of hooves running toward him.

Panicked, he tried to stand, but the pain nearly made him curse aloud. His hip was broken.

Shit.

He looked around for some place to hide. Too late—his instinct sent the warning. Miles looked up and saw a half beast, half man rushing across the mist where he lay.

But the monster didn't land on him. When it crossed the mist his breath caused, it staggered and fell. For a moment, the fiery animal's eyes turned a normal shade of amber. It sighed before turning quiet.

Miles crawled nearer.

"It feels good to rest for a little bit," the half beast said.

What just happened? In his mind—an engineer's mind—a diagram began to materialize as he stared at the creature, seemingly lethargic beside him.

My breath on ancient ice created steam that subdued a half beast. He looked up at Michael and the others still fighting above him. He focused on the orbs hitting each other, causing sparks.

Maybe there's a way to distract them.

His heart pounded, and the need to breathe became overwhelming. He knew he'd stayed too long on this planet. He had to leave. Now.

Miles placed his face close to the ice, opened his mouth, and exhaled.

Amid the sounds of battle, of explosions and screams of madness and anger, there was one cry that almost sounded excited, followed by another and another, until a chorus reverberated against the walls of the crevice and echoed.

"Human!"

Miles lay on his back as the steam from his breath on the ice rose around him. He thought he saw Gaby, Michael, and the other beings staring at him with disbelief. The metallic enemy let out a disgusted scream.

A great multitude of gray mists, half beasts, shape-shifters, and body snatchers descended down the crevice at a dizzying speed toward Miles.

But if his plan was right, they wouldn't be able to harm him.

As the entities dove into the steam rising from the bottom, they surfaced one by one as orbs, gently flickering. A collective sigh rose around him, and then silence fell.

Doomed orbs, doomed souls, Clos Friga, hell, Michael, and Michael's nemesis…

Richelle and their daughter came front and center to mind. He blinked. The grid lines appeared. One dot illuminated, followed by another and another.

What a relief to see the portal!

But his vision started turning blurry. There was no oxygen to inhale.

He was so close to reaching his way home. All he had to do was to crawl in and cross the other side. But he couldn't.

There was no air left in his convulsing body.

30

The sound of chirping birds became louder and louder. Then it stopped, only to resume. It kept going until Miles opened his eyes.

He wasn't sure where he was. It looked like a waiting area of some sort with minimal decor. A large panel of crystal-clear glass from ceiling to floor showcased a beautiful well-designed garden outside. He took a deep breath and paused for a second. Was that the scent of jasmine?

The chirping birds sounded again. He realized he'd woken up on a sofa, and his mobile phone on the side table had been ringing the alarm. He turned it off.

Rafa walked in and greeted him in his natural appearance, wearing the dark gray tunic Miles recognized. "How are you feeling, Miles?" Rafa placed a hand on his shoulder.

"Like I had a good sleep," he replied. He was now used to seeing their slightly translucent appearance.

"You surprised us, Anomaly," Rafa shared as he sat opposite him. "How did you come upon the solution you did?"

"The orbs hitting each other reminded me of atoms colliding," Miles admitted.

"And you used steam to cool them off," Rafa finished his sentence.

"I accidentally breathed on the ice. Then I realized it might work as a distraction." Miles nodded as he looked around and whispered, "Am I dead?"

"You're not dead. You heard your cell phone," Rafa replied.

"Where am I? Is this a spaceship?"

"We stopped using spaceships a long time ago. Wormholes are our preferred means of travel." Rafa smiled as his gaze wandered the room. "You are in what I consider to be the coolest spot on Earth."

Miles raised an inquiring eyebrow.

"This place has an anchored wormhole to Kalumegn. It was installed after Earth was born and will always be here, and its location is camouflaged very well. This is our arrival and departure point from home before we travel to other locations on your planet."

Something in Rafa's reply struck him when he remembered the multitude of doomed orbs. "Is the wormhole from Earth to Clos Friga also anchored?"

Michael arrived as he asked the question. Rafa give Michael a look.

"No, it isn't. But I'll let you and Michael talk. I rarely visit your planet, but you have my assistance, should you need it." With those final words, Rafa left the room.

Miles stood and walked to the window, where Michael stood gazing out at the scenery.

"What you did helped us subdue a convict, Miles," Michael started. "Thank you, on behalf of the citizens of Kalumegn."

Miles nodded to acknowledge the appreciation, but he didn't want to mince words. "I just held my child for a few seconds with my wife in a coma when I found myself trapped in Clos Friga. I didn't want to be there, so I had to do something. I wanted to go home."

"I am sorry, Miles, for the burden placed on your shoulders," Michael stated.

"If Clos Friga is hell, who is your nemesis, Michael? And are you who I think you are?"

"The planet Clos Friga is what humans call hell, where my nemesis, Lucifer, is imprisoned," Michael confirmed.

Miles wasn't sure he was ready for that answer, as a shiver ran through his body.

Michael continued, "We are much different from what you were likely taught growing up. As you can see, I don't have wings. Feathers aren't going to survive flying beyond the exosphere or through a wormhole. I am a citizen of a planet in a different universe. Our planet is of a magnitude that makes Jupiter look cute. And Lucifer is a powerful artificial being."

Miles knew his jaw dropped as he listened, but he didn't care.

"My life is dedicated to fighting this perpetual machine who wreaks havoc on the minds of citizens from different worlds, including Earth, in order to keep its supply of energy—"

"Why does he or it exist?"

Michael lightly waved a hand, and the glass windows began to project images.

"He was built to assist us. We considered him a brother and a member of our planet's high council. He was a brilliant technological masterpiece, but as time passed, he turned on us. He said he wanted more. We thought it was to do more to help, but no, he wanted to rule Kalumegn."

Michael paused and took a deep breath. When he inhaled, Miles saw his luminosity turn slightly brighter.

"It led to civil unrest because a few citizens were on his side. He was sentenced to imprisonment, but he has attempted to escape, as what happened when you were there. Ultimately, it comes to me against him."

The screen changed to show a planetary system and Michael continued. "Clos Friga has no nearby suns, thus no energy source for him. We considered it a sufficient prison where he would languish and decay."

The screen changed again. "Though limited in power, he continued to look for a way to hack into Kalumegn's systems. He couldn't. We tracked each attempt. But in the process, he made contact with other planets and their inhabitants, including Earth."

Miles watched the screen as many hail-like pellets shot from Earth to Clos Friga.

"There is no anchored wormhole between Clos Friga and Earth. Beings who succumbed to his control during their lives, remain in his control as their lives expire. Their life source…the orbs come to him."

Miles remained silent, waiting to hear more.

"This is not an easy existence, Miles, but I'm not going to be defeated. I won't let my planet, or any other worlds he's been toying with, be destroyed." Michael's tone was calm but resolute.

"And I joined the party?" Miles added.

Michael actually smiled. "You are not my understudy. Your life is here on Earth. Admittedly, I wasn't sure about you initially, Anomaly, but you have been a revelation for me, for us, in the council of Kalumegn."

"What happened after I lost consciousness?" Miles asked, curious.

"We reined the bastard in. And we released the orbs into the universe where their energies may find their place. Rafa attended to you here. This is a short window when we can take it easy. Enjoy life as a father and take time to master your extraterrestrial skills. I'll be recuperating myself. But I have to warn you…" Michael paused as dots of light on his forehead flashed.

Miles hung on for his next word.

"Your anomalies have not dissipated. You will continue to see and interact with beings of energy. Since we released a bunch from Clos Friga to the universe, some may find their way back to Earth. Be prepared. You may be called upon to help battle what are unseen to your fellow humans."

Miles nodded. "I'm ready for that."

Michael opened his mouth, but seemed to hesitate.

"What is it?" Miles pressed.

"When Lucifer regains his power, he will seek vengeance against us, and you."

Miles's heart sank. "You waited until this moment to give that warning?"

"Because there is a solution for you, Anomaly. Be patient." Michael produced a small crystal box. "Our, um, chief engineer built a device to cloak your and your wife's existence from him. He will not be able to track you anywhere. And his minions will not be able to link you to what happened in Clos Friga."

Michael held up the crystal box with what looked like a very tiny piece of shiny metal suspended in the middle. "This will bury itself in your body."

Miles stared at it. "I know this is a serious moment, but I'm standing beside an alien who is giving me something metallic to implant inside me…"

Michael suppressed a smile. "You can look at it that way."

"What are the side effects?"

"You will always receive additional screening for a metallic object," Michael answered.

"I can live with that. What do I do now?"

"When you're ready, hold this close to your skin," Michael instructed.

The crystal box floated to his palm. Miles took it and closed his hand. The window display changed once again. This time, it looked like an ultrasound image.

"Your arm," Michael pointed. "You can see it's traveling through you. It will settle at the right spot." Michael's eyes transformed into a pair of human eyes. He looked directly at Miles. "It is good to have your presence on Earth, Anomaly."

Miles gave a slight nod.

The metallic fragment settled somewhere on his shoulder blade, but the ultrasound image brought his thoughts back to Richelle.

"I don't need my wife's heart. I need her alive with me and our child."

"Rafa is taking care of her as we speak." Michael pointed to a door beside the glass windows. It illuminated, then opened. Miles saw Richelle's hospital room. Rafa was in there, taking Richelle's pulse. He looked up and gave them a thumbs-up. He looked familiar in his white lab coat.

"Dr. Dubois," Miles muttered to himself.

"She will wake up soon," Michael said.

He bit his lips and cleared his throat. "Thank you. She's the bravest woman in the universe. Half her heart saved our asses."

This time, Michael's face relaxed and broke into a smile. "Indeed, she is. That's why she is equally protected. A human with no extraterrestrial abilities, and yet her courage pushed you to fulfill the burden of your anomaly."

Miles agreed, but there was something more he wanted to ask. "If I nearly gave up my life in hell, and I'm speaking with an archangel, where is—"

"You have a choice, Miles Penchant. You can stay here and wait for the Magna, or you can return to your wife and newborn."

"That's harsh, Archangel," Miles chided.

"I'm not that kind of angel, Anomaly," Michael replied. "There will be another time to delve into that. Now is the time to live your life."

Miles was back by Richelle's bed. He heard the steady beep from the electrocardiogram machine. The stillness was broken when the door opened, and a nurse walked in and was startled to find him in the room

"We've been waiting for you. I thought you were in the other room where I presented your daughter. That was half an hour ago," she chided.

"I'm sorry. I ended going to another floor to take a break, but I'm back now."

Richelle stirred. The nurse went out to page a doctor as Miles held her hand and kissed her lips.

"I had the strangest dream, Miles, but you made it," she whispered.

"You don't have to worry about those dreams anymore, Rich. They're over," Miles murmured in her ear.

Richelle smiled weakly but clasped his hand tightly. "I know, Miles. I heard your thoughts. I felt it when you were moving around with Gaby…and I know about Clos Friga."

Miles kissed her forehead when his instinct pointed him to two orbs in the room. He looked at each. One was the residual spirit of a former patient. It was simply attached to the hospital floor and did nothing. The other orb looked back at him.

"I'll ask the nurse to bring our daughter," he told his wife.

He straightened and walked toward the door without taking his eyes off the gray mist. As he stared, the gray mist formed a face and smiled at him. It looked familiar.

"Grandpa?" he asked aloud.

"Miles, my boy, it's so good to speak with you after all these years," the old man greeted.

"Your grandfather is here?" Richelle asked.

Miles replied with a bounce in his voice. "Yes, he says he'll stay for a little bit until the baby's presented. Do you mind if I chat with him?"

"Of course not, just don't look too obvious talking by yourself when other people are in the room," she warned in her just-awakened voice.

Miles smiled at his wife.

My little spitfire is back. And together, no otherworldly minion of darkness stands a chance.

###

About the Author

J Elizaga is a fan of science fiction and science mysteries. Born and raised in Manila, Philippines, she peered over her father's shoulders as he watched TV shows such as In Search Of, and Carl Sagan's Cosmos during the 1970s.

J. holds a bachelor's degree in electrical engineering with additional studies in instructional design. She continues to live and work in California.

J. used to write stories during in high school but had set that aside for college and career. That was the case until she attended a writer's conference in San Francisco in 2010. The experience unsealed a door in her mind that she thought had long closed.

J. cherishes the folklore, tales and stories learned while growing up in the Pacific islands, and has taken to writing about fictional characters with extraordinary gifts that supersize their human abilities. Penchant for Darkness is her debut novella in paperback.

Twitter: @jelizaga1
Facebook: @jelizaga1

Reviews

"With this novella, author Elizaga continues her pattern of creating memorable characters with extraordinary gifts based on Pacific folklore. A fast-paced thriller ...enjoyable. " – *Kirkus Reviews*

"An entertaining short story that doesn't get bogged down the details... this is definitely a book worth picking up." – *LoveReading UK*

"A combination of vivid characterization and palpable tension, this slender novella makes for a page-turner... This is a must-read." – *Prairies Book Review*

"... A highly engaging read with plenty of interesting twists and lots of content for its novella length ..." – *Readers' Favorite*

Made in the USA
Middletown, DE
25 October 2020